CECILIA

Linda Ferri

CECILIA

*Translated from the Italian
by Ann Goldstein*

Europa
editions

Europa Editions
116 East 16th Street
New York, N.Y. 10003
www.europaeditions.com
info@europaeditions.com

Translation by Ann Goldstein
Original title: *Cecilia*
Translation copyright © 2009 by Europa Editions

Library of Congress Cataloging in Publication Data is available
ISBN 978-1-933372-87-7

Ferri, Linda
Cecilia

Book design by Emanuele Ragnisco
www.mekkanografici.com

Cover art by John William Godward, *Dolce far niente* (1904)
© The Gallery Collection/Corbis

Prepress by Plan.ed – Rome

Printed in Canada

CONTENTS

For my women friends

CECILIA

PART ONE

I'm fifteen today, and the first light of dawn woke me immediately. Strange: it didn't strike my eyelids but a point in the middle of my body that opened up like a fan, leaving an agitation, a trepidation, like wings beating in my chest.

After all, it's just my birthday, and it can't be the anticipation of presents that's got me so nervous. I'm not a child anymore, even though my mother scolds me for still sleeping with Carite, my nurse, whereas she was already married at twelve. No, unfortunately it's not the prospect of that or other pleasures of the day but something serious—a premonition, maybe an omen, something that a god, visiting me in a dream, announced, or demanded.

It must have been a really cruel god, because I don't remember anything! Not a trace of his features, no sign to identify him by, no order to carry out. Only the message of that anxiety, like an indefinite promise.

Outside, the nocturnal din of carts on the streets has just stopped, while shopkeepers, tanners, and peddlers are not yet calling to customers at the top of their lungs, I don't yet hear the furious hammering of the coppersmith or the carpenter, or the schoolmaster's shouts. In this moment of miraculous silence, when Rome is suspended between night and day, I try to make as little noise as possible while I write, so as not to disturb Carite.

I look at my nurse, I admire the trustfulness with which she abandons herself to sleep: lucky her, she's not afraid of anything, that someone might be saving up unpleasant surprises for her! She has such a simple, generous nature, the mere idea of doing harm repels her. Even though she believes in ghosts, specters, and evil demons, she's sure that divine protection makes her stronger than them: what could she fear from the darkness or from the future? Surely the gods are granting her visions of fulfillment and salvation as she lies there on her side, one hand over her face sheltering her from the early light. And perhaps right now she's dreaming, as she did a few nights ago, that she's a goat, a lovely young white goat who's suckling a little girl, suckling me, Cecilia . . .

She's turning over in her bed, in a moment she'll wake up. I have to hide the papyrus immediately and put off until later thinking about the mysterious oracle that's got me so upset.

I'm in a terrible mood, but I want to try to get over it so I can describe how the day unfolded.

This morning I come out of my room, cross the garden and the peristyle, and there already is the incredibly boring parade of togas filing through the atrium.

Rich and poor, Greeks and Romans, aediles and freedmen, shipbuilders, bakers, carpenters—just as they do every morning, my father's clients have come to pay homage. They all know that this is a special day, the birthday of Cecilia, the beloved only daughter of their patron. They know that, in her honor, the daily *sportula*, the donation, will be more generous. And for this reason alone, from the first in line to the last, they greet me, some kissing my hands and feet, some calling on each of the gods to grant my wishes, some promising to drink a cup of wine for every letter of my name. Hypocrites.

Some of them I know because they are often invited to dinner or do business with my father. The poet Seleucus, who lives on the generosity of his patron, and in exchange recites at every banquet. Flaccus, who hopes—with his support, the respect his name enjoys, and his influential friendships—to join the equestrian order. Alcimus, a freedman of my father's, who manages the wine, oil, and grain trade on our lands: grim, always ill at ease and insecure despite his immense wealth.

And, of course, Pallante, with his heavy beard, the philosophy master, who occasionally stops to talk to me, too.

They all want something from my father or owe him something.

And he?

I go to give him a kiss and already, early in the morning, he seems tired. The office of Prefect of the Annona, who is responsible for Rome's grain supply; the management of his property; the study of medicine (which he refuses to give up, although he hasn't practiced for many years); the dialogues with Pallante keep him constantly busy.

Milone has complained to Carite: from his bed near the door he sees the master studying almost all night long, and so he can't close his eyes, either, out of fear that the master, falling asleep inadvertently, might overturn the lamp and cause a fire. It must be true, because even this morning my father's eyes are red, with dark circles around them. And yet as soon as he sees me he smiles. He abandons the friend whose turn it is to be greeted, and comes toward me, holding out his arms.

"Good wishes, my little lady," he says, hugging me, forgetting for a moment his own duties. And I would like to stay like that, relaxed in his embrace, all day. Instead, casting a disconsolate glance at that stubborn line, he adds, "Go to your mother now. I'll try to be free soon."

I enter her room just in time to hear her cry out. Mirrina, who's combing her hair, has just pulled out a white hair. My mother gets angry if she finds a silver thread that eluded her maid, but she also gets angry when, quickly and decisively, Mirrina extracts it. Lucilla is just like that.

And she weeps for her lost beauty, although to me she is the most beautiful woman.

She didn't realize right away that I had come in, and I leaned in behind her until our two faces appeared together in the mirror.

Her eyes are filled with tears—hard to say if it's because the tug hurt. Lucilla often has shiny liquid eyes, eyes so black they sometimes seem blue. Seeing me, they become even wetter and a tear slides down her cheek. Abruptly she pushes aside Mirrina's comb, then turns, narrowing her eyes as if to get me in focus.

"My daughter," she says, and nothing else. She continues to examine me, while the tears now run copiously down her face. And I feel that in that blurred vision it's not me she sees but a crowd of ghosts: the souls of all her dead children. She's thinking about them, I'm sure. She thinks about them constantly, with a grief that over time has become almost pleasurable.

I embrace her, kiss her forehead and cheeks, as if she were my child. Maybe it's to console her, or maybe to cloud the issue and conceal my discomfort, because it seems to me that on account of them—my dead brothers and sisters—my mother sometimes loves me more, and sometimes less, and when I feel that she loves me less a snake squeezes my heart in its powerful coils, and I would like to shout that it's not my fault if I'm the only survivor, and a girl besides. Instead, now, as usual, I'm careful not to say anything, hiding behind kisses.

She jumps to her feet. As if reproaching herself she shakes her head, the mass of black hair undulating, marvelous and terrible, and says in a tragic tone, "Disperse, shades! And you, melancholy, away, hide your dark face. Let our spirits be filled with joy! It's the birthday of Cecilia, my dear child, who today is preparing to become a woman."

Her theatrical behavior and the pompous artificiality of her words surprise me—could she be quoting some writer?—but the last phrase leaves me really terrified. The tongue always finds the aching tooth, and I am immediately sure that starting today, the very day of my fifteenth birthday, she'll give my father no peace until he's persuaded to find me a husband. Even worse: maybe it's already been decided and they've invited my future spouse to the banquet tonight.

My legs are trembling, but I pretend to be lighthearted:

"Is that a poet you're quoting? Thank you, mother, for those words."

"Don't be clever, Cecilia, I don't like it . . ." she replies, with one of those sudden changes of mood that leave me bewildered every time. Then she sends me away because she has to finish dressing.

Goodbye, my carefree life!

Although vague—hidden behind those few words: "who today is preparing to become a woman"—the threat of marriage darkens the whole day. During the libation to the Lares I continue to scrutinize my parents, but I don't notice anything strange: as always, my father observes the rite meticulously while Lucilla, standing behind him, hands him the incense bottle with her usual slightly irritated indifference.

The dinner in my honor is also spoiled, although the fear that "he" might be there vanishes immediately: on the couches are my friends Domitilla, Lucretia, and Claudia, with their husbands, and my parents' usual guests. The daughters of some of them are sitting on the low stools, but the only male is Duilius, who luckily for me is barely eleven.

I received necklaces, earrings, books, iridescent silks. I have to confess: I don't care about any of it, and I'm even less interested in talking about it—I'm frightened, and I'm sad.

So far I've made an effort to control myself, in order to describe the events of the day, but now I'll say it. And if it were not absolutely forbidden I would shout, in fact I am shouting, pressing the pen into the papyrus until it makes a hole: it was a HORRIBLE birthday. The worst of my whole life.

I think I finally understand why I felt so agitated when I woke up this morning: the dream I forgot contained the premonition of a wedding, and maybe the god who inspired it, knowing that he wasn't doing me any favors, decided to eliminate every trace of himself and of the unlucky oracle. Because there's nothing I want less than to get married: I want to stay here, in this house, as long as possible, with my father and mother, with Carite and Telifrone. Providence willed that I was born into a family that, compared with Lucretia's, Claudia's, and Domitilla's, is like an oasis of peace and freedom. My father is the wisest, the best man. He never seems angry with his friends, he's never raised a hand against me, or his wife, or a slave, manifesting only kindness and tolerance toward us. Even though I'm a girl, he seems satisfied to have me as his only heir, and has always made sure to give me good teachers and an education that many boys would envy. I can use his library at my pleasure; built up over years and years of research, it has so many scrolls and rare and ancient volumes that it's superior to the library in the temple of Apollo Palatine, where the emperor himself, Marcus Aurelius, borrows his books.

As for my mother, it's true that her suffering sometimes seems to become a bad habit, and that fate has given her a nature forever hanging in the balance between fragility and hardness, so that I'm never sure which of the two, mother or Lucilla, I'm going to kiss good morning. But it's also true that she's always been attentive and affectionate, almost too much so.

Only a fool would flee his lucky star . . . And I would be crazy if I were eager to exchange the known for the unknown, the limited but secure freedom I have today for . . . for what?

Lucretia, who's been married for just a few months, is already bored to death in the beautiful prison that her husband, Carvilius Ruga, has shut her up in. She spends most of the day amid hairdressers, seamstresses, and makeup women, and nearly every night she has to go to a banquet with her husband's friends, who are old, like him.

Tomorrow I'll be imperturbable, but now I say: No! My father has to give me more time. And even though it's late I hurry off to knock on his door.

"You're not asleep yet?" he says, and looks up vaguely from the volume he's reading.

I shake my head.

"Have you gargled?"

"Yes, with honey-sweetened water," I lie, to prevent the usual question and to speed things along. Meanwhile I'm rocking from one foot to the other in an attempt to contain my agitation.

"What's the matter with you, Cecilia?" Now his gaze is more intense, darkened by a concern that finally gives me an opening. Without thinking twice I throw myself at his feet.

"I know that my mother wants to find me a husband, but please, please wait. I'm not ready for a step like that, I don't want to live far away from you . . . I wouldn't be a good wife, not yet. Please, I implore you, put it off . . . I'm just asking for a year."

Then I start crying.

He gets up from the couch, grabs my arm, and compels me to stand.

Between the firmness of his gestures and the expression on his face I notice a discrepancy, like a note out of tune, which again seems to offer me a possibility.

"Please, one more year . . . To improve my education . . . my character . . ."

He looks into my eyes, weighs every word.

Then: "Stop crying, Cecilia. When will you learn to control yourself? But all right, I'll think about it . . . Now go to sleep, it's late."

I went back to my room. What else could I do? Carite wasn't there yet. I paced up and down for a while, but I couldn't calm down. Then I took the zither and sat on the bed, just touching the strings with the plectrum, very softly. And I began to sing, under my breath, in my head . . . It makes me feel better. Music always makes me feel better. Sometimes it soothes the mind's turmoil, the way Orpheus tamed the wild beasts with his lyre. Sometimes it draws me into a swirling current that it's lovely to abandon yourself to, a current, or maybe a river, a cascade of light in which I drown, I lose myself in happiness. But singing in your head is difficult, and after a while I stopped.

"All right, I'll think about it," my father said: the same sentence he uttered the time I came home with my hands scraped raw by Master Domitian's rod. I was almost nine.

Do you remember, Annia?

I'm kneeling at his feet, begging him through my tears not to make me go back to school. He helps me up, then leads me into his office, dresses the cuts, and bandages my hands.

At that point Lucilla appears. She bursts into tears and wants me to go and lie down on her bed.

Tossed from one end of the house to the other, I feel confused and lost.

The pain is excruciating, and, rather than soothing it, the salve seems to inflame the wounds even more.

They ask me to explain what happened, though Lucilla is constantly interrupting me, inveighing against that wretched tramp Domitian.

As usual, my father intervenes to soften her contempt, but when I get to the critical moment he doesn't understand why I suddenly jumped up, knocking over the writing desk. Hasn't the teacher often guided my hands as I write? What happened this morning that was different?

I mutter that he was gripping me too hard, hurting me, and,

sure of finding sympathy with my mother, I add that Domitian's hand was sweaty and his breath stank. Oddly, she doesn't take advantage of this to get mad, confining herself instead to exchanging a dubious glance with her husband.

I'm afraid they're beginning to guess my secret, and to distract them I jump off the bed and again kneel before my father. I promise I'll work hard to improve my reading and writing by myself, and, besides, Telifrone, who knows Latin perfectly, will be able to help me. Then I hug my mother's legs and beg her to help me just for an hour a day in the study. Alarmed and perplexed, she makes me get up and embraces me, while I'm still crying.

My father orders me to calm down, then leads me back to the bed. When they are about to leave the room he says only, "All right, I'll think about it. Now go to sleep."

There, the same as a little while ago about marriage: I'll think about it, he says, now go to sleep.

Naturally, I don't rest even for a moment, mind and soul again in turmoil. I imagine them in close council, ready to analyze my every word, to extract the slightest contradiction, my father fighting between the duty to correct my impetuousness and repulsion at the teacher's brutality. I hope he lets himself be persuaded by Lucilla, who now has an opportunity to show openly an aversion she keeps hidden out of the desire to please him.

While I am tormented by these conjectures she comes back into the room. She sits on the edge of the bed, then, her eyes hard, completely dry, she says, "Cecilia, now tell me if Domitian abused you."

I don't know what she means, exactly, and at the same I know perfectly.

Incapable either of continuing to lie or of telling the truth,

I hide my face against her chest. She insists: "What exactly did he do to you? Cecilia, you must tell me. You know that a girl's virginity is her most precious treasure, the most important part of her dowry when the time comes for her to marry."

But as soon as the words are formulated in my mind they rekindle disgust, preventing me from responding.

Then she gets up and leaves the room. I'm so tired I can't think anymore: it no longer matters where she went, or what may be the consequences of my involuntary confession. Curled up in the bed, I sniff, enjoying my weariness and that emptiness in my head. But it doesn't last! Here she is returning, followed by my nurse, who looks like a heifer being led to the altar.

And now? What's going to happen now? I wonder, pulling myself up suddenly.

"You won't feel anything," my mother declares, while Carite is taking off my tunic. But when she starts taking off my underwear I begin to struggle, while Lucilla pins my arms so that she can finish her task.

"You must lie still, Cecilia, otherwise there's a chance I'll hurt you," my nurse orders.

Her pallor and the serious tone of her words convince me that I had better obey. I give in to their actions. My mother holds my legs apart, while Carite inspects the pubis with a finger, very slowly, with a grimace of suffering, as if terror made every perception painful.

Meanwhile I struggle to banish from my mind the image of Domitian, of his hands superimposed on my nurse's. I see him settling on the stool, lifting me up to sit on his knees. Pretending to help me trace the letters correctly, he guides my hand: he squeezes it so hard that my skin begins to absorb his sweat like a slow poison. Then I feel something in my lap: with his other hand, hidden under the desk, he is touching me between the legs, and meanwhile he's moving, rubbing his body against mine.

I jumped up, knocking over the writing desk, sending the tablets flying through the air. Just what I would like to do now, while Carite is still intent on searching between my legs.

Finally, with a sigh of relief, my nurse announces, "She's intact."

As for me, I barely hear Lucilla, who says, as she leaves the room, "Don't say anything to your father. You'll see, he'll decide not to make you go back to school."

Yes, that time Lucilla was on my side . . . She persuaded my father, out of fear that I would lose my most precious treasure in view of that dreaded marriage. But now?

My father will have to be persuaded by himself to put it off.

Whenever Carite comes into the room while I'm writing I immediately hide the papyrus under a book, afraid that she might discover me.

Over the years I've told her almost everything, and yet I don't feel I can share this diary with her. It would be even worse to show it to Pallante, though he expects it. But according to him I should take note of what time I get up, what I eat and drink, my gymnastic exercises, the slightest change in the state of my health, if I've had chills or a stomachache, and what medicine I've taken. Whether I've done my family duties, shown affection for those around me . . . Then he wants me to copy out the fundamental precepts here. So, when he asks me about the diary, I invent a story that has almost nothing to do with what's on my papyruses.

I don't know why, but I'm sure that if I talked to someone about what I write, if I let someone read it, the vein would dry up as if by magic. And I would lose the only thing, apart from music, where I am truly I, and can say what I want, whatever I feel like. My fear of having to get married soon has not completely disappeared, although after what my mother said on my birthday, and my father's famous "I'll think about it," no one in the house has made any allusions to it. But I haven't for a moment stopped watching my parents closely. A change in the way they treat me or refer to me in my presence: no, nothing seems to betray some hidden plan.

For her part, Carite, nagged by my questions, insists that

she doesn't know anything. A few days ago she even added, "If it will ease your mind, when I passed the study I heard the master say to Pallante that he would rather live his whole life on Gyaros, the island of exiles, with his daughter, than a single day without her in this beautiful house in Trastevere."

It's always the same: as soon as I lower my guard and stop worrying, lo and behold someone takes it upon himself to revive my fears. Today it was my tutor's turn. "You, too, will be called on to fulfill your destiny, to insure, through the proper marriage, the progeny of your family," he said. I was so frightened I immediately forgot how angry Aeneas had made me.

So Drusus had finished explaining to me the fourth book of the Aeneid, after pausing, as always, on every unusual word, rhetorical figure, geographical place, and digressing into detailed disquisitions on names and nicknames, on Iarbas and the raging Barcaeans, on verbs, prepositions, and conjunctions . . . Now it's my turn.

Bewildered by all those minutiae that distract me from the story, I begin to recite, taking care only to respect the marks that join or separate the words, indicate accents or pauses. I recite the love of Aeneas and Dido mechanically, my head empty, and that way I manage not to make mistakes, so that Drusus doesn't interrupt me: the passion that is kindled in the Queen, her sister Anna, who inflames it, counseling her to delay Aeneas for the winter, Juno, guardian of marriage, in league with Venus, and then the storm and the two lovers celebrating the sacred nuptials in a grotto.

I recite, enchanted by the music, cradled in an unknown happiness, until, for the first time, I stumble and, stumbling, fully take in the sense of the line: the furious look that Jove flashes on the lovers tears me away from unconsciousness, filling me with apprehension as I read the next line. The father of the gods entrusts to Mercury his orders for Aeneas, and the

Cyllenian, in turn, heatedly addresses the hero: "Are you now laying the foundations of lofty Carthage and, slave of a woman, constructing a beautiful city, heedless of your own kingdom, your fate?"

The Trojan is silent, troubled and dismayed by the gods' reproach and their harsh decree, and, at the same time, terrified at the idea of confronting Dido: how to soothe her, with what words can he tell the Queen, who is mad with love, that Fate commands him to abandon her. In the end he makes up his mind and summons his men: they are to prepare the ships, get ready to set sail. Dido senses betrayal, and heartless Rumor confirms her terrible suspicion . . .

From here on I begin to read quickly, making mistakes in rhythm and inflection. Drusus interrupts me, trying to correct me, to make me repeat, but I can't hear him, too deep in Dido's desperation, too disgusted by Aeneas's cowardice.

At the end, when Iris, with her right hand, cuts a lock of the unlucky Queen's hair, releasing her from her dying body, I throw the scroll on the ground and stamp on it.

Drusus has been my tutor for six years, and he knows me well.

First he says nothing, merely looking up from the crumpled book to stare straight ahead. He waits for me to calm down, then he orders me to pick it up.

"What got into you?" he asks.

"I don't like those lines."

"You don't like the lines of the greatest poet?"

"No, I don't."

"It means that you haven't understood them. All right, let's start again from the beginning. Scan the first line."

I look for it on the scroll and obey reluctantly.

"Now tell me how many dactyls there are, and how many spondees."

I make an effort to count, but I really can't do it, I don't care. Then I say, "Master, it's not the metrics I don't like but Aeneas, who gives himself up to love for a whole year, and then claims he never married Dido in the grotto. He is pious, the poet says, and would like to assuage his lover's grief, would like to console her. Contemptible, that's what he is, talking her head off about Troy, Anchises, and little Ascanius, whom he can't cheat of his new kingdom. Not for an instant does he look at her sweetly, or shed a tear, or show compassion for the grieving Queen."

Drusus looks at me in astonishment. Then, his lips curved in bitterness, he says, "I thought I had taught you something over the years. And if I had put off the study of this marvelous poem until now, it was precisely to enable you to look at it in a more mature way. Instead, you not only express yourself in a vulgar fashion but reduce our Homer to a teller of elegiac little tales, and, what's worse, place the tears and wailing of some woman above a divine duty, the founding of Rome."

"But Virgil, too, would admit I'm right! For example, listen here . . . When Anna brings Aeneas her sister's plea not to leave immediately, to give her a little time at least. Here, listen . . ." and I hurriedly unroll the book, looking for the place:

Thus she begged him, these tearful pleas the desolate sister
Carries again and again: but no tears move him,
No word can he hear with favor: the Fates
Forbid him, and a god seals his mortal ears.

"Look at pious Aeneas, look at him in action! To get him out of trouble, to conceal how hard-hearted he is, the poet has had to resort to the intervention of a god who takes pity and makes him deaf."

My tutor shakes his head: "In spite of your age, you're still a child, Cecilia. And in spite of the education your father wanted to give you and your extraordinary memory, you remain a weak female, incapable of judgment and moderation. I was wrong to think you capable of understanding that we are almost never permitted to live according to our heart. The hero says it himself, the man you heap so much discredit on . . . But you'll understand, oh, indeed, you will. When you, too, are called on to fulfill your destiny, to insure through a proper marriage your family's line—"

"When?" I interrupt him.

"When?" he repeats, confused.

"When will I be called to a proper marriage? Have my parents said something about it?"

"I don't know anything about their plans. But it will happen soon, maybe sooner than you imagine," he concludes, as he withdraws, and from the grim tone of his voice I understand that he wished to punish me.

Drusus's prediction continues to echo in my head, it disturbs me when I'm singing a song, or reading, it disturbs me even when I do my gymnastic exercises, reviving the anxiety that the dream instilled on the eve of my birthday—the terror of what is to come, the terror of what has been.

"The past no longer exists. The future does not yet exist and perhaps will not. There is no reason to torment yourself in the case of one or the other, since they do not belong to you. You possess only the present; you cannot lose what you do not have." I repeated this fundamental precept out loud ten times, and yet it did not soothe me. Things can change so quickly, throwing us into despair, into the deepest melancholy. You know that, Annia, you would say I was right.

It was a long time ago, and yet every gesture, every word is sharply engraved in my memory. It's the keenest of the senses that the omnipotent gods bestowed on me. It's my special eye that sees everything, sees it again, that never closes, never misses anything. It's my ear: it picks up a sound and captures it forever.

I see myself in bed, enveloped in the warmth of the blankets late into the night, happy, lucky, because my father has finally agreed not to send me to school anymore.

And suddenly I see myself in the carriage, as we're fleeing to Umbria, with that happiness in my heart which fate often transforms into anguish.

So I'm in bed, happy and lucky.

When spring arrives the shutters are left open, and the noise of the surrounding streets, the shouts, the laughter, is confused with the voices of my dream, imparting to its events a strange new meaning. A gust of wind shifts the curtain and the light that breaks through is transformed into the fiery chariot of Helios, so that, from the darkness, I find myself contemplating the other half of the sky, already dazzling blue.

Then, suddenly, Carite is tugging at me, and I plunge again to earth. "Wake up, Cecilia, hurry! We have to flee. The master says the plague has returned to Rome."

A little later, as we're getting in the carriage—to me this is a pleasure, an unexpected novelty—I notice my mother's unhappy face. Now that we're ready to leave, and my father is saying goodbye, I suppose in her mind's eye she sees the gentle contours of the Umbrian hills, the transparent air, that whole April countryside of a tender green that strains her nerves, sending her into a deep melancholy.

Especially since my father is staying in Rome to take care of his patients and won't join us till later.

"Later, when?" Lucilla continues to press him.

But he merely repeats that he will come "as soon as possible," in a tranquil tone that that day seems to be more exasperating to her than usual.

As the carriage is setting off, Lucilla, her voice moving suddenly from apprehension to an icy hardness, says to him,

"Paulus, take care of yourself, please. I don't want to find myself a widow, and at the mercy of my father."

Then she lets the curtain fall and says not another word.

Mirrina, on the other hand, won't stop cursing the Christians, who, with their impiety and their terrifying rites, have provoked the gods' punishment and the spread of the infection.

Sitting between Carite and Telifrone, with Ossus lying at my feet, I avoid paying too much attention either to Lucilla's gloom or to the macabre conversation of her maid, which would spoil my good mood. I'm looking forward to the adventure of the journey, the excitement of sleeping all together in the carriage, the joy of being at the villa, with its large spaces, the freedom to go in and out as I like, expeditions into the fields with Quintus and Marta.

I abandon myself to every bump, every abrupt stop, crashing into Carite and Telifrone, ending up with Mirrina on the opposite seat, or falling to the floor, on top of my dog.

"What is there to laugh about, foolish Cecilia," my pedagogue rebukes me, pulling me up by the arm. He, like my mother and Mirrina, seems to be in a terrible mood.

The jerks, the jolts, the noise that comes from the street make him nauseated, and every so often, pale and panting, he shifts the back curtain and, in spite of his fear of the plague, sticks his head out to get a breath of air. I kneel on the seat beside him and take advantage of the opening to look around.

We haven't even left Rome, and the Via Flaminia is packed with carriages, oxen, mules, and people on foot.

A cart drawn by two horses and driven by a man in a cape who is shouting at the top of his lungs passes a carriage and is right behind us. Intent on observing the driver, who keeps shouting, I don't realize right away what he is carrying. A rag knotted around the driver's head covers his nose and mouth, making his words incomprehensible. Our coachman slows to let him pass. And then, as he goes by, I see: I see the dead piled up in the cart, and, in the midst of the bodies, in the grip of delirium, a man who is gnashing his teeth, kicking and punching to free himself from a corpse that is lying, face up, on top of him, pressing down on his chest.

"But he's alive," I say, filled with anguish, to Telifrone, pointing to the man.

"Not for long . . . He must be in the last stages of the infection," he whispers, even more ashen-faced.

"Where are they taking him?"

"Down there, maybe," and he indicates a field beside the road, where soldiers are standing around a smoking pyre.

I watch the cart as, passing us by, it jolts on into an alley, heading toward the fire. Then my pedagogue closes the curtain with a brusque gesture and orders me back inside.

I return to my seat next to Carite, who notices how pale I am and asks if I feel ill. I shake my head, without a word. I can't erase the image of that living man among the dead from my sight, or, from my mind, the fear that he'll be thrown onto the pyre before the breath of life leaves him.

I start praying for him, and for others like him who may be lying in that suffering heap, buried under the plague-ridden corpses. I pray to Proserpina to work quickly, to hurry from Hades to cut a lock of his hair and deliver him to Dis.

I pray to Mercury to fly to the soldiers to tell them that the unlucky man is not dead. I pray to Jove the father to cause a rain so heavy that the flames are extinguished. I pray to Aesculapius to cure him. Finally, in confusion, increasingly disturbed and no longer knowing which god to invoke, I appeal to the benevolent and nameless god my father always speaks of. And I hope that the man who is about to die was pious and virtuous in life, so as to deserve his intervention.

Afterward, I feel somewhat calmer. But during the night, shut in the carriage with my mother, Carite, and Mirrina, I wake with a start from an agonizing vision: a man is writhing on the pyre, screaming, and already the shining whiteness of his bones is visible, when a winged creature arrives, whirls three times around the pyre, and then vanishes into the dark air, abandoning him alive to the flames.

My forehead drenched with sweat, I wake Carite and tell her the dream.

"Don't worry about the infected man—he'll certainly die first. I'll tell you who that man on the pyre was," she whispers bitterly. "That lying wretch Tallus, it was, who got me pregnant and then betrayed me, and, still not satisfied, two years later swore up and down that the dead child was not his. He spent the nights carousing and playing dice with the soldiers returning from Syria in the escort of Lucius Verus. He caught the plague. And I can tell you that even when he was tormented by the blisters and fever he kept promising and lying. If he's still burning, it serves him right. Don't think about it any more now, sleep."

And Carite turns over.

The vengeful tone of my nurse's words increases my distress. I've never heard her talk like that.

I wonder how it's possible to dream about someone you've never seen or heard of. Or maybe, I think in surprise, the good Carite called down a curse upon him, and the gods used me to tell her that it had been fulfilled. According to what my father says, neither pyres nor other torments await the souls of the wicked. So where is this Tallus?

In other words, I spend the rest of the night trapped amid these and other painful questions, and at dawn, when my nurse comes to wake me, she finds me wide-eyed with anguish.

You see: from happiness to distress in a single day. If that's the way things go, in a month I could be married to an old man who is fat, boring, and maybe even mean. Do you realize that, Annia?

L uckily Lucretia, escorted by Acme, her favorite maid, came to see me this morning. I say "luckily," because she took me out of my thoughts. But she also gave me a new worry.

I see her approaching through the garden with an excitement that neither her *stola* nor her matron's veil can mask. She immediately insists that we go off to a secluded spot, and then, unable to sit still for a single instant, blushing and wringing her hands, she confides in me.

A young man has just told her he loves her.

I'm writing it like this, to get to the point. Lucretia, on the other hand, gets jumbled up in the story, confusing the before and after, letters with roses, porticoes and the theater with the arena. She leaves out the names of her lover, her husband, and her father, calling all three "he," so that they won't be heard by who knows what indiscreet ear. One moment—face red, eyes shining—she seems at the pinnacle of happiness; the next, pale as a corpse, she's practically tearing her hair in despair. On top of everything else, Acme keeps breaking in, adding a thousand details and acting as if she knows more than Lucretia.

In other words, I just can't figure it out, and so I tell her to sit down and start the whole thing from the beginning.

She sinks into a chair, then sits there in silence, her hands trembling, her breath short. She seems on the point of fainting, but finally she gets control of herself.

Although more comprehensible, the story is still interrupted by so many sighs, exclamations, and interjections, invocations to Venus, to Juno, that I can't report it faithfully. Besides, even if I could, I'm afraid that, written down, it might seem ridiculous, and I really don't want to insult my friend. So I'll cut her off: I'll speak in her stead.

About a week ago she was walking under the portico of Octavia with her maid. In a bad mood, she avoided looking at the works on view there, as if, rather than cheering her up, the Venus of Phidias, the Amor of Praxiteles, and the Alexander of Lysippus would deepen in her, by contrast, a painful feeling of emptiness. So she glanced around cautiously as she walked, in the hope of finding in a fashionable hairstyle or a ruby pin some detail that might spark her interest and distract her.

Suddenly, she noticed a tall, nice-looking young man, half-hidden behind a column. For a moment their eyes met and he smiled at her, then he disappeared into the crowd. A little later he reappeared, a few steps in front of her. If Lucretia stopped, he also stopped. Now he preceded her, now he followed, now he was beside her, performing a sort of dance amid the columns. She pretended to ignore his moves, but neither the candor of his smile nor the liveliness of his gaze escaped her.

In the end the young man was hailed by a friend and stopped to talk to him.

The following morning, in great secrecy, Acme delivered a letter filled with sweet words, promises, and entreaties. It seems that Aurelius (this is the young man's name), besides being handsome and enterprising, knew how to demonstrate his ability in the art of eloquence: never boring, never vain or sententious, but, rather, simple, passionate, and tender.

She was so struck by the letter that she answered it, with expressions of refusal, however, and pleas to leave her alone. Yet she couldn't stop thinking about him, when, a few days later, she met him at the theatre. Feeling a persistent gaze that caressed her shoulders, she turned and saw him.

The young man smiled at her, then moved forward a few rows. He applauded every dance step enthusiastically, and shouted when the actress performed a scene of passion. And meanwhile he kept turning around, speaking to her with his eyes, imitating each of her movements, while Lucretia appeared distracted, pretending not to notice anything when in fact she noticed everything.

The next morning, when she woke, there was a rose outside the door of her room. The same evening, she was invited to a banquet with her husband, and again encountered Aurelius. By a strange coincidence (or more likely thanks to the complicity of the host), they found that they were neighbors at the table. He took advantage of this to whisper flattering words and stare rapturously at her, eyes sparkling. He touched the cup that she had touched and drank from the part where she had drunk. He did the same with the food, and then brushed her hand.

In addition, he was solicitous toward her husband, letting him drink first, offering him the garland that had been offered to him, agreeing with everything he said.

While my friend is relating all this, I am invaded by misgivings. There's something oddly familiar about what she's saying that at the same time makes me suspicious.

Acme's attitude also seems strange. Although she doesn't say anything, she giggles and blushes, displaying an excessive involvement in the story.

I don't say anything to Lucretia, because I wouldn't know what to say, and I merely advise prudence. After all, she is a married woman and there are big risks. This recall to reality inspires a new wave of emotions: sometimes she trembles with fear at the idea of being discovered by her husband, or, even worse, by her father; sometimes she seems to have forgotten their existence entirely, and, without the least reticence, sighs as she praises the young man's voice, his hands, and his eyes.

Finally she thanks me for my advice and promises she'll get rid of him at the first opportunity.

As I watch her hurry off, I'm sure she's going to throw herself into the arms of Aurelius.

Alone, I continue to think about her words. I'm sure I've heard them. But where, and from whom? No one has ever told me a story like that, neither Carite, nor Telifrone, still less Drusus, my mother, or my father. And so?

Suddenly a line comes mind:

"Be the first to touch that cup which she has touched with her lips . . ."

I jump up and head for my mother's room. At the door I call to her, to make sure she's not there. Then I go in and pull out from under the bed the trunk where she keeps the forbidden books.

I rummage around, opening and closing the scrolls, and finally I find the right one. I skim the lines, reading here and there with increasing rage. I roll it up again in a hurry, shove the trunk under the bed. Then, with the book hidden in the folds of my tunic, I hurry through the tablinum, avoiding the stern gaze of my ancestors, and shut myself in my room, to write a letter to Lucretia immediately.

My dear friend,

Maybe what I'm about to tell you will pain you. If that's the case, you should know right now that I'm sorry about it, but the idea that my revelations will prevent greater disappointments and torments consoles me. So I'm summoning my courage to share with you what I've discovered, transcribing the following lines from a poet, Ovid, whom you may not yet be familiar with. (I've underlined the passages that seem most important.)

Wax spread on the tablets
Gives a start to your steps; precedes you

With your thoughts; carries caresses
and *imitates* the phrases of lovers,
and you, whoever you are, *don't be sparing with
prayers . . .*
and *make promises*, because so long as you promise,
you suffer no harm; promising,
every scoundrel becomes a millionaire.

If she walks under the vast porticoes
Idly, you too idle and waste
Near her your time; and now pass her,
Now follow her steps; now go quickly,
Now more slowly. And don't be ashamed
of following her in between the columns
or putting yourself at her side; and let it never be
that she can sit without you,
beautiful and pleasing, among the people crowding
in the concave theater. The spectacle
she offers you with her beautiful shoulders.
There you will be able to look at her and admire her
as much as you want and speak to her with your eyes!
Let every gesture of yours be a word!
Applaud if a mime on the stage
dances, shout aloud your support
to those who play scenes of passion.
And when she gets up, you too rise,
sit as long as she sits: at her whim
for her consume all the day.

You must see, dear Lucretia, what an imposter that Aurelius is! A real scoundrel! Worst of all, he hasn't got an ounce of imagination, seeing that to woo you he has to follow a manual, however poetic. Just imagine, I even found the banquet scene, almost exactly the same as what you told me: he drinks from the cup at the same point where you drank, he brushes your hand, and then tries to please your husband. Even the description of the letter he wrote corresponds: no trace of pedantry or vanity, he is to use only tender, simple, believable words. But the poet repeats many times that his suggestions are meant for winning free women, certainly not married women like you. My dear friend, please, be careful: don't compromise your dignity, don't expose yourself to danger, letting yourself be deceived by a frivolous, insincere man.

Farewell.

I gave the letter to Mirrina's daughter, to be delivered immediately to Lucretia.

On the one hand, I feel relieved that I've put my friend on her guard; on the other, a doubt still torments me. In order not to wound her too much I in fact avoided transcribing a passage that, as I think back on it now, seems to me decisive: the one where "the soldier new to the weapons of love" is exhorted by the poet to corrupt the servant, to seduce her straight away, "because every risk is nothing, when with the mistress the maid is complicit and shares the guilt."

I read and reread. I return in my mind to Acme's strange behavior: first, the excitement with which she continuously interrupted her mistress, providing new details about the young man, then that silence, pierced by sighs and laughter, as if the story involved her directly.

Unfortunately the truth by now seems naked and pitiless. The deception of Lucretia is complete: surely Aurelius has already had her maid.

A little while ago, with Pallante, I applied myself to practicing attention.

"You are endowed with a truly uncommon memory, Cecilia, but more important than memory, or any poem or philosophical text you are able to repeat perfectly, more important than any other faculty—I was saying—is attention. Try always to be vigilant, present to yourself. You must know and fully intend what you are doing at every moment, so that you will always have at hand the fundamental rule of life, the distinction between what depends on you and what does not."

I feel I've already broken the rule. Does it depend on me if Lucretia is captivated, and by a scoundrel? Does it depend on me if she's bored with her husband and if Aurelius is insincere? I seem to have interfered in affairs that have nothing to do with me, but I certainly can't tell Pallante the whole story. So, approaching it in a roundabout way, I ask:

"Is it really wrong to behave as if nothing were extraneous and indifferent to us?"

"Of course it is, because it doesn't correspond to the truth. Does it depend on you that you are an only daughter? That your body is subject to illness? That you may have around you people who act in an unjust or spiteful way? That your father is Prefect of the Annona?"

"On me no, but on him and my mother, certainly! You don't know how many difficulties, how many problems they had to overcome to obtain that post . . ."

"Well, again you're mistaken. Honors depend not on us but, rather, on the magnanimous will of Caesar."

Partly what he says is true, and partly it's a lie, coming from someone who from morning to night is pledged to pay homage to his protectors. But what can I do? If I continue to argue he'll say that I'm a female and for that reason the path of wisdom, even if it's accessible, will turn out to be more arduous.

So I say nothing, and he starts again: "Does it depend on you that the family you belong to is noble and wealthy? If you don't recognize that these facts are outside your control, if you consider free the things that by nature are enslaved and what is extraneous your personal affair, you will suffer, you will be troubled, you will complain of gods and men.

"On you it depends, however, to be fully satisfied with what happens in the present, to act justly, or in a manner consistent with reason, and to love those around you with all your heart."

I wonder if, putting Lucretia on her guard but without completely revealing Aurelius's deception, I have really showed that I love my friend. I look at Pallante, I sigh.

Then, to change the subject, I say:

"Master, why don't we read the philosophers anymore?"

"Cecilia, how many times must I repeat: you talk too much . . . You get distracted by words, by a thousand questions, instead of concentrating. And then, do you want to study Heraclitus, Plato, Epictetus, and Zeno? Do you want to fill your head with complex and subtle theories? You'll do it later, when you're ready. For now the essential thing is to respect the maxims I've provided. And you'll acquire that respect through the various forms of meditation, the development of a logical dialogue with yourself—through the diary, for example . . ."

He pauses, scrutinizes me, and for a moment I'm afraid he's going to ask to read the papyruses. But he must not think they're too important, for he resumes, "As I was saying, Cecilia, you must know and want fully what you do in every instant, so as never to lose sight of the distinction between the things that are subject to your power and those which are not. You mustn't separate yourself from this principle when you're sleeping or when you get up or when you eat or drink or converse with others."

I nod, then am silent for a long time, pretending to reflect on his words, while I'm still tormented by having hidden the truth from my friend. I just wish he'd go, but he sits there for I don't know how long, with his eyes closed and a look of absorption hovering on his face. Maybe he's sleeping, and without disturbing him I leave the room.

Always treat others with tolerance and kindness. Never give a sign of anger or any other passion, remain at the same time absolutely impassive and affectionate. (Think of the irritation and contempt that Aeneas roused in you and how you acted toward your teacher, think of the book you threw on the floor and trampled, offending him! Think of the intolerance you show toward Pallante.) Look at yourself as at an insidious enemy, correct your character, you're not a child anymore: regulate your excesses, your foolishness, the anger you've displayed since you were small.

Yes, all right, correct them, but preserve the only virtue that so far you seem to have been supplied with, that is, sincerity.

I love my father.
I love Telifrone and Carite.
I love Annia.
I love my mother.
I love my friends, and even Drusus a little.
The crowd on the street, the passersby, the common people, foreigners. I don't know them, they are distant from me, they are indifferent to me.

Yes, I love my mother.
I don't love Lucilla.

May my mother forgive me, but sometimes I just don't understand Lucilla. When her attitude changes abruptly, and in the same sentence she calls me first "dear child" and then right afterward a woman, so that she may soon get me married, so that she will be rid of me. Or like that night so many years ago when, in a burst of madness, she decided to change our lives . . . All by herself, on her own. All in a night.

It's still dark, I wake confused, not knowing how much time has passed since the morning of our flight from Rome or where I am. Slowly, however, by the light of the moon, I begin to distinguish the fresco next to my bed: the yellow of the pomegranates on the branches, the rustling of a turtle dove's wings among leaves rippled by the wind, and, half hidden by a tuft of grass, a white rabbit almost identical to mine. I'm finally in the country, in my room, and I sigh with happiness.

I call Carite, but there's no response from the empty bed. And because I'm thirsty I get up, groping for the water pitcher. That's not in its place, either, so, letting memory guide me, arms outstretched, I go out of the room in search of my nurse.

The moonlight shines between the columns of the peristyle, casting bands of light and shadow on the floor at regular intervals: the shadow so deep that it seems ready to swallow me up whenever I step in it.

In the center of the garden, the tritons of the fountain blow into their shells, raising to the sky a threatening sneer.

It's strange how night transforms this lovely place, how it mutes sounds and shapes. Now that the noise of the slaves at work in the fields and barns has faded, along with the placid chewing of the animals at pasture, the villa is immersed in a silence as dense as the shadow I'm crossing.

Suddenly, under the portico, the familiar statue of Diana of the Woods seems to aim her bow right at me, while I hear a wolf howling in the distance. I walk faster, heading toward the study, where the dim light of a lamp filters out through the curtain.

I don't immediately recognize the male voice engaged in animated discussion with Lucilla, and I hold my breath, listening: now the man is wailing, with accents of rage that distort his words. Then my mother says, "There is no point, Ilus, in tormenting yourself," and I understand that it's uncle Julius. What's he doing in the villa? And when did he get here?

Instead of calming him, Lucilla's advice provokes a crisis. Afraid that they might notice my shadow I stand motionless, but to tell the truth I'm petrified by the violence of the scene that is unfolding just behind the curtain. I see the silhouette of Julius, who paces the room with long strides and then throws himself to the floor, pounding it with his fists between curses and sobs. I grasp some fragments of a sentence, words with a brutal and obscene sound that I've never heard and whose meaning I don't know.

My mother is kneeling beside her brother, she is about to embrace him, but every so often that fury seems to become contagious, and she in her turn explodes in cries and curses. Then I realize that they are talking about Claudius, my maternal grandfather, who died last night.

He had been sick for years, and had been near death many times, only to recover. I seldom saw him, since he lived in retirement in his villa in Etruria, but from the rancorous stories my mother tells I got a frightening image. He used to beat his wife and children bloody, and she died aborting her third child after he kicked her in the stomach.

Besides having a hot temper, he was fiercely avaricious.

My mother told me that when Julius was of age, his father, instead of taking him along to the Senate and helping his career, kept him in a state of humiliating dependence, grudging him every sesterce, and forcing him in the end to go into debt illegally, a situation that my father rescued him from at the last moment.

Even though many details of my grandfather's history are mysterious to me and I don't completely understand what Julius and Lucilla are saying amid their sighs and laments, I can still grasp its profound meaning, as if the scene, filtered through the drawn curtain that obscures the gestures and muffles the voices, delivered to me alone its pure, concentrated distillation of hatred.

My uncle is now talking about a certain Aulus, a scheming opportunist who, after flattering Claudius with a thousand visits and gifts, got himself adopted by him shortly before he died. He also says that Grandfather changed his will, and now he fears for his inheritance.

"The important thing is that he is dead. If he changed the will in favor of Aulus, we'll get it annulled. We're free, Ilus," my mother comments.

"I am free, since I'm not yet twenty-five and am about to marry as the law requires," my uncle answers, "but you'll need a guardian in order to inherit . . . Lucilla, you don't have three children."

There is a moment of silence, then with a firm voice my mother retorts:

"I have five children, and don't you ever forget it, Julius."

She approaches the curtain, ready to leave, and I run away as fast as I can, not knowing that that last phrase of Lucilla's is destined to change our lives. For the worse, naturally.

Luckily no Pallante today, so I devoted myself to practicing my zither, which I love like Ossus, or maybe a little more, like Carite, only in a slightly different way.

It accompanies me, responds to me, growing closer and more vivid. Then my voice begins to rise up, expanding, making body and soul vibrate. It eliminates boundaries, dissolving them into a vast, eternal order, in which I am no longer I and at the same time truly I, released into a warm and luminous immensity.

There I am practicing my singing, when again the miracle, at once expected and surprising, takes place: suddenly I feel serene, distant from myself, from nature, from the world, or perhaps completely the opposite, absorbed into the hidden substance of things, truer and better.

Emptied of feeling, and yet at the peak of happiness, I see Lucretia and her maid coming toward me. Except that the excitement of the other day has been transformed into something much more violent: in the blink of an eye she is standing before me and, without even giving me time to greet her, she starts in breathlessly, furious:

"How could you! How dare you write such outrageous things, insinuate such lies about the truest man in the whole city, the best creature in the world? How could you do this to me? I've always thought of you as my best, my most trusted friend. And yet you went so far as to invent lines by that poet Ovid, who if he existed really would deserve exile, for all the malice he puts into his so-called art. I asked myself why you acted like that. I thought and thought and the answer, most unfortunately . . . What is the answer? The only possible answer? Well, however sad, however disappointing, there is only one answer: what drove you was envy. You're envious of me, because I'm wooed and loved, while your father hasn't been able to find you the slightest trace of a husband . . ."

I interrupt, calmly insisting that the truth is I'm the one who doesn't want to get married, I'm terrified by the tedium and the lack of freedom, which, besides, she is well acquainted with.

"Old maids all talk like that, while the real problem is your bad character, which everybody knows. Everybody, that is, except me. Whenever Claudia or Domitilla accuses you of being spoiled, restless, impulsive, pedantic, obstinate, I, like an idiot, defend you."

At least three times, in a tone that is sometimes contemptuous, sometimes pathetic, Lucretia concludes her tirade and starts it all over again, adding small variations to the account of the facts, stuffing it with hyperbolic examples, and interspersing knowing pauses, theatrical gestures and expressions, eyes turned to Acme as to the great public of the Forum, to win its approval. It's a superfluous stratagem, because the sly maid merely nods. I'm surprised, but evidently my friend has been listening to her father prepare his cases for the prosecution and has learned the art. Whatever I say, she twists it against me. So I say nothing. No one is blinder than someone who doesn't want to see. Love must be just that: an illness that strikes like lightning, distorting your senses, an illusion, similar maybe to the illusion that the men in Plato's cave fall under, who think they see reality but in fact perceive only its shadows. A madness like the one that possesses unlucky Dido, convinced that the sole source of life resides in the very man who will lead her to death. While I'm absorbed in these thoughts Lucretia stares at me in annoyance, as if my attitude were unjustly depriving her of pretexts for losing herself even more thoroughly in her mirage. I sustain her gaze for a while, resisting the challenge, making an effort to remain imperturbable.

"For once, the little schoolmistress is at a loss for words!" she comments in satisfaction.

A moment later I say spitefully, "Words are useless with you, Lucretia. And since love of the truth was never your strong point, I would rather not tell you everything I know about the truest man in the world."

Unprepared for my counterattack, she turns her back, and for a long moment doesn't move.

Now what's going to happen? One thing is certain: even if she's dying to know, she will never condescend to ask me questions about her lover. In fact, followed by her maid, my friend goes off without even a glance, and doesn't notice Mirrina, who just then is crossing the garden, limping ostentatiously.

Spoiled, maybe I am, right, Annia, you who know who I am, you who see me, but does it depend on me? Or on my father? No, it depends on the bad use I make of what he gives me.

Restless and impulsive, yes, certainly. Does that depend on Lucilla, who never finds repose, and who just today, incapable of simulating the ritual of violence at the celebration of the Matralia, chased Mirrina out of the temple of Mater Matuta so vehemently that she fell and sprained her ankle? No, if my mother is restless and impulsive it's up to me not to follow her example. I will pledge to control myself for at least three days, not be confused by my mind's impulses or by false appearances. For at least three days I will try to restrain my anger. I promise you, Annia.

Pedantic? Have I turned into vanity the joyful lightness that books have always given me? Into exhibition what germinates and grows only in the depths of heart and mind? Into illusion poetry, into empty consolation or admonitory speeches the works of the philosophers, into pride the power of music?

Have I shown myself impatient and arrogant toward those less educated than me? Did I offend my friend, showing off my knowledge of a poet unknown to her, on a question that touches her to the quick?

Obstinate. Yes, very obstinate.

Spoiled, restless, impulsive, pedantic, obstinate. Certainly Lucretia doesn't know all my other flaws, otherwise she wouldn't have mentioned only those.

What can I say about the SPITEFULNESS that I displayed today, implying that I know more than she does about the man she's in love with, hinting at a suspicion that is bound to torture her?

Once, in the past, I gave extreme evidence of that spitefulness, causing the death of an innocent person. You're the only one, Annia, who knows it.

My mother discovered the papyruses.

I don't know how she happened to notice that "The Art of Love" was missing from the trunk of banned books, but she came rushing into my room like a Fury. I watched her without comprehending, while she rummaged in every corner, tossing things in the air. Finally, she found, along with the poem, the hiding place where I keep the scrolls. She dragged me into the study and, in front of my father, began to read passages randomly, walking up and down, and letting the sheets fall to the floor one after another.

"Do you hear what this ungrateful daughter says, this shameless girl who describes in minutest detail her states of mind as if they were the most important thing in the world? She lies to Pallante, who is called boring and hairy, says she fears marriage more than the plague, dares to claim that I, her mother, abandon myself with pleasure to grief for my four children, then goes on at length about Lucretia's sinful adventures . . ."

I felt the pain of profanation, every word a stab. Trembling, holding my breath, I waited for her to get to the point where I wrote that I didn't love Lucilla . . . Instead, she abruptly broke off, flinging the rest of the scrolls to the floor and trampling them. Then she gave my father a challenging look.

"Here is the result when one insists on educating a daughter like a boy . . . What do you intend to do?"

He stared at her for a moment, then looked at me thoughtfully, for a long time. I know that look, which says more than a thousand words. I know it so well, and am about to fall to my knees, as usual, but even I have some sense of moderation, or rather I want desperately to have it, for love of him, and so I contain myself.

"What are these scrolls, Cecilia?"

"It's only a diary, father . . . of a kind . . . Even Pallante advises me to give an account of my days and to take note of the fundamental precepts . . . in order not to forget them, to improve myself . . ."

"And in your view what does Lucretia's adultery have to do with fundamental rules?"

"I put her on her guard, I tried to dissuade her."

"Enough," my mother interrupted. "You two would be capable of spending hours dissecting all the most abstruse details. I know what has to be done." And, picking up the scrolls in her arms, she threw them on the fire.

My father leaped up. For the first time I saw something that resembled anger alter the lines of his face. His voice shaking, he said only, "Leave us now, Cecilia."

And I fled the study anticipating the moment when the anger of that gentle man would fall on Lucilla.

Even if I have been very careful not to tell my teachers anything about my extraordinary senses, in order not to be accused of presumption, they recognize that I have a good memory. Day after day I rewrote what Lucilla had read and then burned. Even when I found mistakes or inaccuracies I rewrote the same, identical sentences, just as they were stamped in my memory. In revenge: although my father later forced us to a sort of peace, I consider that I ended up the winner. The pact is the following: Lucilla must allow me to keep a diary, while I pledge to respect the suggestions of my philosophy teacher, without digressing or pausing self-indulgently on my states of mind.

As I was rewriting, I realized that my father is right: it's true that I get upset at every breath of wind, am constantly at the mercy of my feelings, even when my intention is to understand something about them.

But now I can't stop, the words evoke other words, as if these papyruses, animated by a demon, had a life of their own. If magically they also managed to write themselves I would be spared a lot of labor. But they evidently need my hand—all of me—as an instrument.

All I can do is bow to their command and proceed with humility and strength of mind in this undertaking. Even though I don't think I'll be able to keep the promise I gave my father.

Today Carite announced the good news: no villa this year, we're staying in Rome for the whole summer.

"Why? What happened?"

"Nothing. The mistress says she's too tired to face the journey."

To check on the situation I go and see Lucilla.

In fact she seems paler than usual.

"I'm sorry, Cecilia, to make you stay in the city, too, but I'm feeling very weak. Your father thinks that the move would make my condition worse. Maybe you could visit Claudia in the country for a few days."

Yet again I wonder if my parents are plotting with a view to my marriage, but the feebleness of my mother's voice convinces me that she isn't well. Seeing her like that, now that I've defeated her, I feel sorry for her, and can't help embracing her. I tell her to rest and not worry about me, staying in Rome doesn't bother me at all. It's the absolute truth: for a reason that I haven't yet explained, the idea of going to Umbria doesn't make me happy the way it used to. In fact it oppresses me: just tonight I had another vision of Quintus. And then I'm always afraid of seeing Marta. Over the years I've continued to avoid her.

But now the hazy heat, made even more stifling by smoke from the fires that are constantly breaking out in the city, forces me to stay in my room. Every movement is an effort, so I can't find anything to distract me from remorse for my spitefulness. Since the day we quarreled, Lucretia has disappeared, yet all I can do is think about my friends. We've been close since we were little. Or at least that's how it seems, now that that basic trust has been broken.

What happened, I wonder? And why?

In spite of our differences—that Lucretia always wanted to get married (even to someone like Carvilius Ruga), while I'm still hoping to put it off; that she doesn't understand how anyone can live in Trastevere ("a valley choked by the bad river air"), while in my view its very proximity to the river and its uncrowded spaces, full of gardens and vegetable plots, make it the most beautiful area, not to mention that we live in a true *domus* and she on the ground floor of a four-story apartment building, even if it is on the elegant Caelian—in spite of this and other differences, there's always been a bond between us, until now.

I've always loved her gaiety, her imagination, maybe frivolous sometimes, but free, almost daring. Yes, her playfulness has often been a comfort to me, lightening my gloomy moods, smoothing the rough edges of my nature.

With Claudia, on the other hand, I've always enjoyed our similarities, our affinities of taste and perception. Ever since we were children, we could understand each other at a glance. Lately, the seriousness my friend and I had in common has been changing in her to severity, almost hardness. She considers the slightest complaint or expression of discontent to be improper, claiming that one should control one's impulses and always appear serene and detached. Every day she's more like her mother, who spent the day with distaff and spindle, weaving with her own hands her husband's toga, and tunics and cloaks for her children, who dutifully helped her husband with the libations to the Lares and Penates, and worshipped Roman divinities so ancient they were unknown even to Numa Pompilius, yet with a cold and slightly false piety.

Two years ago, Claudia married Manlius Cornelius Dentatus, a descendant of the ancient family of the Cornelii, and
since then she has observed the traditions of her ancestors with
an austerity that to me seems rigid and artificial, and insensi-
tive to emotion.

What can I say about Domitilla? That particular aptitude
for seeing things in their true light, which kept her from yielding to any flattery from men or situations, over time has been
transformed into disillusion. Bitterness has set her mouth in a
painful curve. Now that her father is struggling to find her a
husband, Domitilla, while impatient to be married, is aware
that she's not very pretty, and has been going around the
Forums wearing a tight belt that emphasizes the thickness of
her waist, and with her hair hanging loose and untidy around
her pudgy face.

She seems to display every defect as a provocation. Now I
feel guilty when I'm with her, not only for being slender and
well proportioned but even for having both legs! If something
good happens I scrupulously avoid telling her. Instead I report
to her in the minutest detail what has afflicted or annoyed me,
although I know that not even this will save me from her poisonous barbs.

But maybe my friendships with Lucretia, Claudia, and
Domitilla, if I really think about it, harbored from the start the
seeds that are now corrupting them. And maybe, Annia, you
know already that I am fated to remain alone, to lose or destroy
those I love.

Quintus: his skin golden as the rays of the sun, his feet swift as the wind. Perfectly balanced on the slippery rocks, or stretched out full length, ear glued to the ground to eavesdrop on the moles at work, intently digging their tunnels. It seems to me I can still hear his blackbird's call, an imitation so exact that a real blackbird answered every time. He didn't know how to read or write; he knew all nature's secrets. He had nothing. I took from him everything.

Again that fatal spring of six years ago. Sounds and images strike me with the force and vividness of the present. The plague-ridden man who is thrown on the pyre. The voice of Lucilla saying, "I have five children, and don't you ever forget it."

And now I see myself in the villa's belvedere, with my pedagogue, who is reciting Homer. I am impatient for him to finish so I can go find Quintus and Marta: I haven't seen them since we got here.

As soon as Telifrone concludes with an "All right," I jump to my feet . . .

You must not go far from the pasture, swim in the river, or play leapfrog in the streams, be careful not to disturb sleeping snakes or look for bees' nests, don't walk up to oxen and heifers from behind . . . Again I seem to hear his warnings drifting off into the air as I run around the garden, pass by the villa, the farmer's house, the slaves' and overseers' courtyards, get beyond the infirmary, the barns, and the stables. Now in the open country, amid vineyards, olive groves, and flowering peach trees, I stop to catch my breath, focusing my gaze in the direction of the meadow, and the majestic oak beneath which Quintus and Marta are usually taking shelter from the sun: two pale spots that today, too, are visible in the dense shade.

I start running again, shouting their names, while the silhouettes of the siblings wave their arms in greeting. I reach them panting, bathed in sweat: although it's April it's almost as hot as summer. Quintus is bare-chested, Marta has rolled the sleeves of her tunic up over her shoulders.

I say, "Hello, Marta. Hello, Quintus." And they answer, "Hello!"

As always, the conversation breaks off, because though the siblings know some Latin, I know only three or four words of their dialect. But rather than limiting our intimacy, the language barrier seems to reinforce the deep core that beats within us, where the bittersweet taste of blackberries mingles with the sharp scent of figs.

They immediately take me to see the newborn calves. Maybe to test me, to demonstrate that nothing has changed between us despite the months of separation, first Quintus, then Marta sticks an index finger in the mouth of a calf and stares at me, waiting. I quickly confirm our friendship by imitating the gesture.

Quintus is twelve, Marta eleven. So they're a little older than me, and they decide what we'll do. And I ask nothing better than to trust in my friends, in the freedom they allow me to discover, far from Rome, far from Telifrone, who wants me to walk like a dog on a leash, without looking around. Here, instead, my gaze can get lost in the horizon, or observe the tiniest things: a skillfully woven swallow's nest, a drop of resin that has imprisoned an ant, the perfect geometry of a spider . . . "Look," Quintus says every time. "Cecilia, look."

He gives the signal, and starts running, away from the cows. Marta and I follow him along the slope, toward the river.

The rule is that you can't stop. Anyone who violates this has to walk barefoot among the nettles. But the Tiber is quite far and I am short of breath. I stop often, while Marta tries to drag me by the arm and Quintus turns, laughing, without interrupting his run. When I reach them they have already dived in.

Panting, I collapse, flat out on the pebbly bank, eyes closed, until I'm hit by a violent spray of water. I jump to my feet and find myself facing the siblings, who are splashing me wildly. I attack in turn, and for a while the battle rages.

Then we all lie down in a shallow spot.

The smooth surface of the pebbles caresses our backs, and the water penetrates our ears, making us deaf to external sounds, while amplifying the sonority of the river.

One of Quintus's hands accidentally brushes mine. He seizes it and clasps it for a long time, to seal that moment of happiness. Then suddenly he gets up, out of the water, and from the bank starts shouting my name as he points to a strip of green where clumps of nettles are poking up.

I don't move, pretending not to understand that the moment has arrived to pay the penalty. Marta says something to her brother, perhaps asking for mercy. But Quintus insists. He continues to call, "Cecilia, Cecilia!" while I plunge my head under the water so that I can't hear him anymore. I know I have to respect our pact: if I don't, something will change between us forever. And yet I cannot. My wet tunic seems to weigh like lead and obstruct every movement. Or is it my will that holds me back—an arrogant will, almost a challenge? The knowledge that that young slave cannot compel me to do anything?

Just then he jumps into the nettles, and begins to trample them with a sort of furious joy. To demonstrate his courage? To humiliate me? To pay the penalty in my place, so that our pact will not be broken?

Suddenly he trips and with a cry falls down.

I have a moment of uncertainty: that last gesture, might it, too, be part of his strange performance? But it's only a moment, because immediately afterward I see Marta hurtling toward him, then bending over, trying to pry away the hands that her brother is gripping tight around one foot. I get up and, stumbling among the pebbles, run toward them.

And then I see. On the sole of his foot I see the snakebite: two deep holes, perfectly incised.

A deathly pallor has spread over Quintus's face, while fear and bewilderment make his eyes bigger.

With a sharp stone Marta is already digging out the wound, then she brings her lips to the swollen foot. She sucks the poisonous blood and spits it out with frenzy and precision, in the grip of an icy madness. She signals me to go to the villa for help, but, seeing me immobilized, she yells something and gives me a push.

I start running, pervaded by an anguish that keeps me from getting tired. At times I seem to be flying, as if Mercury, moved to pity by my friend's misfortune, had tied his winged sandals to my feet.

Quintus begins to vomit in the cart that's carrying him to the infirmary. He complains of thirst, then, as soon as he drinks, he's attacked by horrible stomach pains.

Latrus, the slave assigned to the infirmary, administers a compound of great theriac to which he has added ground viper's tails.

I insist on writing to my father, but Latrus says it was he who recommended that remedy—the only one that's sometimes effective. Nothing more can be done for Quintus. We can only wait, trusting in the capacity of his body to recover.

But soon my friend is seized by a violent convulsion: his heart pounds as if it would crush his chest, then suddenly stops. Or gasping for breath, he raises his head, his mouth open and twisted in the struggle to breathe.

I go and see him whenever I can evade Telifrone, who allows me only one visit a day.

I take his hand and hold it tight between mine.

When the poison seems to give him a little respite he turns toward me, observing me from an infinite distance, and yet with sadness, a sadness that penetrates my heart like a knife.

Then I join Marta in the meadow. Sitting on a rock, we're silent, mesmerized by the rhythmic pounding as she beats the ground with an olive branch.

One evening, when Quintus has begun to vomit up blood, I go to my mother's room and cry in her arms.

"Children die, too, my children died, too," she says, and hides her face in my chest.

The next day Carite wakes me, telling me that Quintus has died.

My father, arriving from Rome, takes him away from his companions and orders that a proper funeral rite be performed.

He is an orphan, and the washing of the corpse is entrusted to Marta and the two slaves who shared their rooms.

Laid out on the pallet, his feet facing the door, he lies in the room for two days. His friends open his eyes and close them, put the coin for Charon in his mouth, then burn incense on an altar behind him. Marta watches over him for two whole nights.

At dawn on the third day, a small procession escorts the bier to the cemetery. While the torches shine transparent in the light of early morning, the name of Quintus is invoked for the last time and the casket lowered into the grave. His sister lays upon it his olive stick, and I am about to add a slingshot that I made with my own hands, but I feel a sudden impulse of shame and hide it behind my back.

Then Marta, my father and I, Telifrone, Latrus, and a dozen

slaves eat eggs, chicken, bread, and salt. We throw the remains around the casket and return to the villa in silence.

The next day, with my pedagogue's help, I want to compose an epitaph.

He suggests that I write: "He lived in the fields and was happy."

But the phrase seems too simplistic, in fact hasty, as if Telifrone had no desire to waste time reflecting on the life of a country slave.

Suddenly the epigraph seems to compose itself in my mind. I repeat it to him so that he can help me express it well. In the end I write:

"Here are commemorated the Remains of Quintus, a boy who lived only twelve years because of a girl's carelessness. But his soul is blessed and will not go among the shades. The sky and the stars have welcomed it."

Accompanied by a slave who is a skilled stone carver, we go to the cemetery. But already, in the crude, hesitant strokes of someone who doesn't know how to write and is struggling to copy, with upside-down letters, made almost indecipherable by rage, these words have been carved in the stone:

"Quintus, a twelve-year-old slave, bitten by a snake died after seven days."

I hide in the storehouses, among piles of grain and amphoras of oil, to escape the hostility that even the most familiar places seem to display. Then when someone comes looking for me, those very places seem unrecognizable and alien. I feel relief only in the moments when (secretly, because now it's absolutely forbidden) I can join Marta in the pasture.

During her brother's days of agony, at the news of his death, during the funeral rites, she didn't shed a tear. Now, too, she sits on her rock, eyes dry, intently striking the ground in front of her with a new stick. As I approach she gives me an expressionless look, then goes back to rhythmically beating the tortured grass.

Faced with my inertia and distraction when it comes to studying, Telifrone only worsens my misery, saying that I am just the typical stubborn girl, disobedient and foolish, and that he had warned me about the danger of snakes.

For her part, Carite, when she hears me weeping in my bed at night, comes to sit beside me, and, holding my hand, whispers incomprehensible litanies, whether prayers or magic formulas I couldn't say.

From Lucilla I get no comfort: seeing my tears she reacts as if at a signal and starts to cry silently herself, a silence that counters my grief with hers, making them incommensurable.

How is it possible that no one around me is able to offer the slightest consolation? Without knowing why, I shun words, walling myself up in a torment that sometimes takes my breath away.

Then one morning Telifrone says that my father is waiting for me in his study. For the first time, I am terrified at the mere idea of being in his presence. What's happening to me?

And yet I am utterly certain that only the man I'm afraid of—that is, him—will be able to save me.

I rush to the study and throw myself in his arms. He holds me tight for a long time. Then he begins to speak. He says that death is not an evil: it's not a good, but it's not an evil, it's simply the work of nature. And there can be nothing bad in what is willed by nature. Grief over Quintus's death comes from my girl's weakness, my incapacity to understand that death is merely the dissolving of the elements that we are made of, and that are destined to change into other elements. In order to help me he says a lot of other things whose meaning I don't grasp and that perhaps he himself doesn't believe. He says that death can have different meanings. But if in his eyes Quintus's death represents an economic loss, and in mine an emotional one, we are both wrong, because the boy's life never belonged to us, and now it is simply restored. For the young slave it is, rather, a liberation. The gods have set him free. Why then grieve so much, why not rejoice in his fate?

When I say nothing, my father observes me at length, then adds, "But maybe there's something you're not telling me, that you're not telling even yourself? This is the moment to look into the depths of your soul, Cecilia."

Then I seem to understand the terror I felt at the announcement of his summons. My father will oblige me to discover the source of my pain. He has the authority and the tools, and just now he has decided to make use of them.

With unusual coldness I evaluate his affection for me. Will it be great enough to bear a truth that seems to me unspeakable?

Then I meet his clear gaze, which is so kind, so gentle. In the state of mind of one who, forced to jump into the void, trusts in the saving intervention of a deity, I place my trust in him and tell him that I was the cause of Quintus's death.

Only when he considers that he has calmed down, my father says, "I intend to ascribe such foolishness to your extreme youthfulness. If it gives proof of an ignorance perhaps inevitable in a girl, it nevertheless contains the seed of a greater sin, which, on the other hand, does worry me.

"A great philosopher, Epictetus, would tell you, 'You are a little soul carrying around a corpse.' And this little soul, which supports a body fated to disappear in a short time, claims that it can alter the natural order of all things. In presuming to be able to subvert the design of providence, this soul shows its impious pride.

"Quintus didn't die on account of you, because you broke your pact, refusing to pay the penalty or other such nonsense.

He died because that is what god established. Everything that happened to him, from the beginning, had been set aside, among the things of the universe, to be assigned to him and interwoven with his life. Do you understand, Cecilia?"

I nod, struck by his severe tone. Then, more mildly, he continues, "We must do our best: always, in whatever circumstance, but without pride, indeed, humbly, modestly, always recognizing the possibility of error, and shunning that permanent dissatisfaction with ourselves that can only spill into vice and sometimes superstition. Take the return of the plague to Rome. Even among my patients of rank and culture there are those who, yielding to emotional impulses, demonstrate an excessive fear of the gods and, presuming to be at the center of the universe, consider the illness that afflicts them to be punishment for their own sins. You do the same when, accusing yourself of the death of that young slave, you mistakenly judge it an evil: but it is neither an evil for him nor a misfortune for you. On the contrary, you will be fortunate if you withstand grief and bear it with nobility."

A few days later he returns to Rome, to his patients, and I'm alone.

If I happen to see myself again at the river, head under water in order not to hear Quintus calling, I immediately rummage through my mind for my father's words.

I have no guilt, it was god who decided my friend's fate, and used me to bring it to fulfillment. I was only an instrument. To presume that my actions can change the plan of providence is foolish, as well as impious.

If, against my every wish, I am assailed by new doubts and ask myself under what order Quintus was assigned such a fate, or who is the distant god I am to worship, without even knowing his name, I dig my nails into the palms of my hands in order to stop thinking about it.

Then Telifrone says it's time to resume the story of the Odyssey.

But instead of returning to the point where we left off, he goes, without explanation, to the book in which Odysseus, having arrived at home in the guise of an old beggar, has just defeated the thug Irus and responds to the suitor Amphinomous's wishes for happiness:

The earth nourishes nothing frailer than man,
among all that breathes and walks upon the earth.
Yet he ever thinks that one day he will be able to overcome evil,
as long as the gods give him strength and his knees are agile;
when then the blessed gods give him sorrows,
these, too, he bears, if unwillingly, with a constant heart:
because thus is the mind of men upon the earth,
as the father of gods and men inspires it day after day.

My teacher stops and, refraining from his usual commentary, says that we'll stop here for today. He goes off, leaving me alone to reflect on Odysseus's words.

If I perceive a note of sadness, unusual in Athena's protected hero, I also recapture an echo of what my father said.

I realize that Paulus and Telifrone, each turning to the treasure he holds most precious, philosophy and epic, have tried to offer me comfort. But no matter how I struggle, the meaning of the words seems to escape, fly away, dragging my soul into the void.

And now even seeing Marta hurts me. The look that she gives me when I join her in the meadow, without expression, without a trace of blame, wounds me.

One day, I simply stop going there.

I've started to write again after a week of interruption, or maybe I should say refusal. The mere thought of the papyruses closed up in their hiding place oppressed me. I was oppressed by the guilt that they now concealed, a vivid torment thanks to my overdeveloped senses. I felt their presence—like an intrusive cry—whenever I entered my room.

At night I was assaulted by terrible visions of my friend covered with blood, and I woke in a sea of tears, convinced that the gods wished to punish me.

During the day I continued to talk to Pallante, my heart in a vise that in his presence I couldn't release.

After the pointless hour spent with him, and after my lesson with Drusus, I mostly stayed in my room.

I lay on the bed with a book, but I couldn't concentrate and soon gave up. To soothe my anxiety I repeated my father's words and those of Odysseus about destiny, I repeated them one by one as I had been doing over the years, whenever I woke up in a sweat from a dream about my dead friend.

It was in those moments in particular that I heard the call of the papyruses creeping into my whispers. I heard them utter my name in a faint, sepulchral voice.

"Cecilia . . . Cecilia . . . We're here, don't forget about us. Come! Pick up your pen! We're waiting for you."

One morning when I woke up, they annoyed me so much that I took them out of their hiding place, determined to throw them on the fire, as my mother had done. Then something stopped me, a thought that Pallante would consider silly: if I destroyed them I would erase every trace of our lives, all the more precious just because they are ephemeral. Apart from the honesty and the learning of my father, which the records of the Annona and the treatises on medicine might preserve, what would be known of the rest of us, of our feelings, our hopes? Lucretia's guilty love for Aurelius would have vanished forever, like my mother's ageless mourning, and the terrible death of an innocent boy.

Your name, Annia, along with your portrait, would perhaps remain, carved in the marble of your tomb, but all the evidence of your life, like the yearning I still feel for you, would have disappeared into nothingness.

No, I couldn't destroy the papyruses. Even if time took care of that, or, more likely still, the many who consider every word of a woman vain and outrageous.

The next day, at any cost, I would start writing again.

I want to talk about my mother, of the zeal with which she's taken part in the rites of the Matronalia. In March, during the Matronalia, she went to the temple on the Esquiline to offer flowers to Juno. Last month when she celebrated the Matralia she violently chased her maid out of the temple of Mater Matuta. And yesterday, in spite of her weakness and the heat, she went out again with Mirrina to celebrate the Nones of Caprotina, bringing Juno an offering of milky sap from the fig tree.

This outburst of piety surprises me: in fact I remember always noticing the indifference, almost apathy, with which she worshipped, as if it had nothing to do with her.

What's happening to her? Maybe she's worried about her health and, no longer trusting in my father's remedies, is asking for divine aid? Or does she have a more intimate prayer to address to the goddesses of women, maybe hoping to be pregnant again?

I prefer not to think about it.

Yesterday, utterly unexpectedly, Lucretia came to see me.

As soon as I see her she seems different. Her gestures, from which every trace of frivolity and pride has disappeared, are light and quick, like the ascents and swerves of a swallow.

When we embrace, asking each other's pardon, I almost feel that her body is losing substance, growing thinner in an extraordinarily fragile yet powerful palpitation.

Her eyes are no longer flashing with fear but show a different light, warmer and gilded, that, along with hope, expresses a new, finally realized happiness. A joy that is yearning and yet fulfillment. Then, suddenly dimmed by a veil of abandon, that light fades, as if marking the surrender of her whole being to a divine force. Then I feel her drift off: a grain of sand in the middle of the sea, a grain that is everything and nothing. If Lucretia moves me with her fragility, at the same time I admire her, even envy her, because I feel she's part of a truer, more beautiful reality, from which I am excluded.

So Love's arrow has struck her.

She couldn't talk about it to anyone else, neither Claudia nor, still less, Domitilla. And yet she absolutely has to talk about it, not to dissipate her treasure but to assure herself of its existence, to be certain that that grace, that blessedness, that resurrection are not only a dream.

Quietly she tells me things that I can't repeat exactly—I'm so ignorant I can't even imagine them. She whispers about myriads of kisses, ecstasy, languor. About hollows and cavities, secrets of her body that she didn't know, whose existence her husband can't even conceive of.

How mysterious the time of love is, she sighs, and how it flies, dissolving the days into hours and the hours into minutes. The time of love is mysterious and cruel, profound and fleeting, for the end always invokes a new beginning, again and again, while already night is falling and she has to hurry home.

How she hates her luxurious prison now! How she hates the husband she never loved! At night, when she hears Carvilius approaching her room with his weighty, unsteady tread, she pretends to be asleep. He tries a gesture, a caress, then gives up. But once he climbed on her anyway and took her. A few minutes of torture, and he fell asleep. Lucretia threw him off her like an old blanket.

In order not to be separated from Aurelius, every day she invents a new illness to delay going to the country with Carvilius. She doesn't care about being found out. She doesn't care about her father's name or even his anger. Still less about her husband's name and his anger. Let them appeal to the law, repudiate her, send her to prison! Let them kill her, piercing her breast with the sword!

She says she is ready to pay with death, so dear to her is her sin, so sacred it appears to her eyes.

While Lucretia continues, gentle and tragic, I don't know what to do but listen in silence and feel ashamed. Armed with that poem of Ovid's, with his elegant words, I almost kept the miracle from happening. "Love of truth has never been your strong point," I was even stubbornly mean enough to tell her, and instead she, without the help of books, without the spur of grammarians and philosophers, has found the truth in love. Found herself in another, recomposing the original harmony.

I want to tell her that I understand, even if it's not really the same, and that sometimes at night, a moment before going to sleep, or when I'm absorbed in music and singing, I feel a lightness in my body, as if a part of it had been detached. It's a strange sensation, a buoyancy that expresses both emptiness and presence: the body of my dead sister Annia, her soul that survives in me, light as the breath of life. This union that endures disembodied, this love, is me, Cecilia, stripped of my visible wrapping: it's solitude, yearning, and at the same time the memory of having once been two.

I want to say all this to my friend, but then it just seems like abstract thoughts, far removed from life, from the fulfillment that beats in her heart, and I say nothing.

When Lucretia left I felt like playing. But I quickly realized that the Greek melodies weren't having any effect.

The notes faded into the air, one after another, without blending into a whole. Cut off from their profound unity, I heard the sound as if I were separate from it: my soul perceived it as cold and distant. The very state that Telifrone always recommends to me, because, according to him, it allows us to maintain our freedom.

So that my pedagogue wouldn't hear me, I went and shut myself in the most remote room of the house and sang some simple popular verses, inspired by an ancient fable, which I adapted to the zither: the lament of Psyche, who, wounded by Cupid's arrow, now burns with love for Love.

Slowly, what my friend's words had only allowed me to guess at took shape through my voice, the inflections I gave Psyche in love sometimes sorrowful, sometimes light. It was a tender melody that excited my soul and my senses, pushing them to the point of abandon, until I felt a yearning vibrate inside me—a cord stretched between heaven and earth, between salvation and ruin.

Later, as I was about to fall asleep, I heard it again, increasingly sweeter and taut, while a hand caressed my breast and thighs, touched my pubis. I was at the height of this tension when Love lifted me in flight.

Then I saw countless stars shining over the earth, I saw the sun fill the space with light, marking in its daily course the confines of day and night and in its yearly course the rhythmic succession of summer and winter.

I saw the gentle light of the moon, the reflection of encounters with its brother. Now hidden, now high over the earth with its full orb, waxing or waning according to its phases, always different. I saw the five planets trace their orbits in the opposite direction from the rotation of the sky: on their slightest motions hung the fate of peoples, and the greatest events, like the smallest, were subject to the influence of a good or evil star. I admired the masses of clouds, the rain, the flash of the lightning, and the thunder of the heavens. Content with looking upward, I then lowered my gaze to the earth and suddenly woke up.

This morning Carite gave me some news that both excites and terrifies me. My suspicions were well founded: my mother is pregnant again.

A little late, I offered prayers to Bona Dea, Mater Matuta, Cybele, and Faustina Minor. A little early, I prayed to Carmenta, Juno Lucina, and again Mater Matuta to watch over her and the child at the moment of birth. Then I quickly got dressed and hurried to her room.

Lying in bed, pale, with an unusually timid expression, she suddenly seemed much younger. She stretched out her arms, but as I was about to hug her she stopped me: "Gently, Cecilia, be careful." Then, holding my breath, I bent my head so she could kiss me.

"Now you understand why I couldn't help keeping you away from your beloved countryside," she said.

I was about to say that it didn't matter, that instead the news made me very happy . . . But she raised a hand, interrupting me.

"I don't wish to talk about it anymore, Cecilia. And I would like you to observe the same silence. Your father has ordered complete rest, which means staying in bed for the rest of the pregnancy. He's also forbidden all contact with the outside world, all sources of fear or displeasure, any hint of anger. For that reason, my daughter, please behave in a mature and responsible way, don't do anything that might worry me. Will you promise?"

I nodded, and she sent me away with a kiss.

I went to the garden to play with Ossus. Although he is now a dog of six, he has the impetuousness and thoughtlessness of a puppy. My white rabbit died a long time ago, and yet Ossus still looks for him. Even today, when he saw me, he began scrabbling among the hedges and digging holes, barking the whole time. With a start, I thought of my mother, and instructed him to be quiet, but as usual he didn't obey. In order to quiet him, I had to leave him alone.

I'm again remembering the extraordinary dream of a few nights ago.

On the wings of Love, I saw the whole firmament in flight: the stars and the planets, the clouds and the lightning, I heard thunder and then pounding rain. What can this vision mean? And Love, what does he have to do with it? What did the god mean to tell me? It reminds me of a passage I read with Drusus, from Seneca's "To Marcia, on Consolation," in which the philosopher, inviting the interlocutor to imagine the moment of his entrance into life and choose whether to cross the threshold or give it up, evokes everything he would see: the firmament, in fact, and all the marvels of the earth—plains, mountains, rivers and streams, vast seas furrowed by ships in search of unknown shores. I don't remember what comes next, so I go to the library to look for the volume.

"You will see that man in his audacity leaves nothing untried and you will yourself be the spectator and a protagonist of mighty undertakings: you will learn and teach the arts, some of which serve to maintain life, some to embellish it, and others to regulate it. But there, too, will be found a thousand plagues of the body and the mind, and wars and robberies and poisonings and shipwrecks and changes of climate and of the body, untimely grief for those most dear, and death, whether an easy one or only after pain and torture no one can tell. Think about it, weigh your decision carefully: if you would reach these wonders, you must pass through these perils."

And now suddenly the dream is clear to me.

The god is announcing a birth.

Flying among the stars on his winged back was not me but my sibling, on the point of deciding whether to enter life. But why was it Love who showed him the world? Inciting bodies to join with his inescapable arrows, might he be the first among gods, the source of all life, because of whom every reality exists?

All my siblings come to mind.

Before me: one miscarriage, then Flavius, dead at six. After, a stillborn male, and then you, Annia, my sister, who died at the age of five, when I was seven. I see clearly your golden curls, which are startling amid our smooth dark heads. Your deep dimples, in your cheeks and your fat hands, into which I thrust small rocks. Your unsteady running and sudden stumbles. I hear your laugh, hoarse and strangely deep. One by one, your toys appear to me: the terra-cotta rattle, the horse encrusted with blue glass, the rag doll that you wanted to call Cecilia, and finally the sparrow that was always with you, until the end.

I hear the sound of our games: nuts colliding on the stone bench, the ball thudding on the gravel, marbles banging. My shouts as I try to teach you to read the numbers on the knuckle-bones and you get muddled and in the end annoyed, and throw them all up in the air.

I see you as you slip out of your bed and come to mine, and, afraid of the dark, hug me with an extraordinary force that almost frightens me.

Annia, it's the first time I've been able to evoke your image, just as today is the first time that I can write the memories I have of you without giving in to a pain that's too much for me.

For three days and three nights you fought fever and delirium, stricken by a disease that neither our father's remedies nor the Egyptian scarab that Carite had hidden under your pillow could vanquish. On your forehead a repulsive flowerlike spot appeared.

At night, in my bed, I hear you call my name in a voice I don't recognize. "Annia, I'm here!" I answer, running to your room. But I always find our father barring my path. Only a slight trembling of the lips betrays his torment as, in a calm, flat voice, he orders me back to sleep. Then I hear our mother's footsteps leaving your room and running to hers.

From there comes the echo of her cries, the crash of objects hurled on the floor or against the walls.

At dawn on the fourth day, Annia, your soul left you.

When they let me see you, with the flower of vivid red carved into your forehead, you're holding your sparrow in your hands. They all forgot about him, or maybe no one had yet dared to separate you.

Your hands, which always welcomed him like a nest, have been transformed into the bars of a cage, and, eyes closed, he's trembling all over. Then I pry open your fingers, and the sparrow rises: first, in an unsteady flight, he makes two or three circuits of the room, bumping against the walls and ceiling; then finds a way out through the door open onto the garden, and up he climbs above the pines and is lost in the distance.

If our father was wrong and you had not dissolved. If your soul hadn't passed into the air, becoming transformed, expanding and exploding, to be reassumed into the seminal mind of the universe.

If Telifrone, too, was wrong, who believes that the soul at death goes into another body, and your soul, Annia, had not been reincarnated in a new living being, perhaps a puppy or a boy, but anyway not you.

If I was right, and what remained of you was that light breath that I sometimes feel mingled with mine.

If, then, Love could return to show you heaven and earth, revealing to you not the fate of men, which is sometimes lucky, sometimes unlucky, but your own brief life: Annia, would you again choose to be born? A fleeting carefreeness, against three days and three nights of agony?

Annia, forgive me for having left you alone in the dark that you were so afraid of, just before you died.

This morning, in a more energetic state of mind, I went to say good morning to my father, as Pallante was leaving after their daily conversation.

Kissing me on the forehead, he said in a worried tone, "You're pale, Cecilia . . . Do you not feel well?"

"I'm shut in the house most of the day and I can't even play music without feeling nervous about disturbing my mother."

He looked at me gravely, perhaps ready to reproach me, and instead, with an unusual impetus, ordered, "Hurry up, find a maid to come with you. We're going to the port. The last ships are arriving from Egypt."

Ah, father, my savior . . . What would become of me without your tenderness and love, even if I'm not always the way you want me?

I threw my arms around his neck and then went to find Carite.

In the end it was Daphne who came with me, because my nurse, on Lucilla's orders, was still busy polishing the silver.

Here I am then on a beautiful morning in the Kalends of September on the wharf of Trajan, along with a young servant who is getting her first view of the sea.

Heedless of the port traffic, of the hazardous maneuvers of docking, of the incessant procession of dockers unloading sacks of grain from the ships, deaf to the cries of the men weighing and checking the goods, Daphne is not silent for a moment, assailing me with the silliest questions: What in the world are those white crests dancing on the water in the distance? Is there a waterfall down there, at the far end, beyond the line that divides sky and sea? And if so, where does it fall? Might there be another sea, or an immense lake, that all that water empties into?

First I try to answer, then I order her to be quiet.

My father prepares to officiate at the sacrifice of thanksgiving, and around us the workers have stopped, bowing their heads in prayer. As soon as I see the horns of the ox appear I lower my head. Not because I'm so devout but because sacrifices always seem unbearably horrifying. The desperate gaze, the snout raised to resist the rope, the front legs planted: the beasts know, when they are led to the altar. Perhaps my father is right, maintaining that they are not endowed with reason. As for the soul, though, from which every good or evil gesture comes, I am certain that they possess one, and no worse than ours: swans bring food to their parents, elephants are faithful to their vows, and even ants bury their dead.

Even with my eyes closed, I can painfully distinguish every sound, so, just the same, I see my father, head covered, tossing grains of barley on the altar, cutting a tuft of hair from the victim's forehead and throwing it on the fire. I hear him invoke Ceres and Neptune, and while the music of flutes rises I hear the axe crush the animal's neck, hear its agonizing death rattle.

I keep my eyes closed for I don't know how long. When I reopen them it's all over: the guts have disappeared from the blood-stained altar and the meat has been carried off for the banquet. I move a few steps away, taking deep breaths, while around me the frenetic activity resumes.

Now my father is talking to the group of men who came to see him as soon as we got out of the carriage. They must be his minions—I think I've seen some of them in line for the morning salutation. In all that hubbub, they listen to him with deference. From time to time he points to the ships, from which grain for Rome streams without stopping. Then he approaches a functionary whose job it is to record on a papyrus the quantities weighed. All he does is write and affix seals, but as soon as he is aware of my father's presence he forgets everything and bows low, an act that impresses me. For the first time I'm struck by the idea that my father can inspire fear. I observe them attentively as they speak: to tell the truth, it's my father who speaks, while the functionary merely nods nervously. They go on like this for a while until, at a sign from the prefect, my father, we head toward the storehouses facing the channel.

Here other complicated operations get under way: the grain is transported to the bank and loaded onto oared boats, barges or ferries meant to reach the Tiber and go up the river, under sail or towed, to the port of Emporium, below the Aventine. My father explains all this while, shoved this way and that by porters, measurers, and ballasters, I see the first boats loaded with goods moving slowly, hauled by bands of men on the quay. I've never seen so many boats, so many people at work, so many sacks of grain in my life.

"Does all this grain go to Rome?" I ask.

"It certainly does," he answers. "The spring harvest is enough for only four months. This comes from the storehouses."

For the first time my city seems to me like a giant with an insatiable belly and, at the thought that my father is directly responsible for appeasing its hunger, I am invaded by distress: if there isn't enough grain in the storehouses, will he be blamed?

Hungry people will surround our house, waiting for him to come out so they can pelt him with dry bread. Because Paulus is a doctor, after all: what can he know about Egyptian wheat, sea and river transport, the storage of grain?

I remember my mother the day the Emperor Marcus Aurelius, before leaving again for Germany with Commodus, summoned him, to entrust to him the post of Prefect of the Annona.

Paulus, although he certainly couldn't refuse, did, however, remind him that he had no experience in administrative matters of such importance, with the well-being of the entire population of Rome at stake.

It seems that our prince made a gesture with his hand as if to dispel every doubt. He then invoked his reputation as a good farmer and outstanding family man, so competent, scrupulous, and responsible in managing his own properties and those of his wife that he had increased his wealth by honest means. A reputation that was, besides, confirmed by the pre-eminence of his studies and his irreproachable service as a magistrate.

In other words, Paulus could only bow and thank him.

But now what if the grain from Egypt turns out to be insufficient again, if famine strikes Rome? I almost regret the absence of Pallante, who certainly would say that these are not things that depend on my father.

The appearance of a tall man with a curly beard who is wearing a senator's toga distracts me from such thoughts.

After exchanging an affectionate greeting, the two begin to discuss the quantity of taxable goods, if they are greater than, the same as, or less than those of the preceding years. My father utters his name, and I realize that this is Ennius Severus, the Prefect of Grain Distribution, whom my parents always speak of with respect. Then they go off, absorbed in conversation.

When they return, Ennius, examining my face, says, "So, you are Cecilia."

Uneasy, I immediately bow my head.

"Ah yes, she is my daughter," my father confirms, while I remain mute.

"Well, then," the prefect comments, in a vague, distracted tone that is at odds with his sharp, fixed gaze.

This morning I was practicing the zither in front of Telifrone when I heard him sigh softly.

I stopped to ask what was wrong.

"That song . . . We always sang it at home," he replied sadly.

I'm used to his melancholy, the way I'm used to the white pallium that he takes off only to put on another, identical one. But today I sensed something different behind the mask, so for the first time I asked him, "Do you really miss your homeland?"

I didn't have time to regret my indiscretion before Telifrone burst into tears. I felt a mixture of pity and embarrassment that made me uncomfortable, and not knowing what else to do I kept standing up and sitting down again, like an idiot, without looking him in the face.

Then, slowly, he got hold of himself and, drying his tears, said, "I regret having yielded to such a reprehensible outburst in your presence. Such an example of weakness should not come from your pedagogue. Cecilia, I swear by your Juno that it will never happen again." Instead of comforting me, that firmness of purpose echoed like a ban, an unjust exclusion. What a moment before had inspired intense embarrassment now kindled my curiosity: suddenly I realized that I knew almost nothing about my pedagogue, the person who, with Carite, had been closest to me from early childhood.

So I persisted, asking him what had caused his outburst.

He didn't answer right away. He gazed at me, hesitant and thoughtful, then he said, "All right, then. However hard it may turn out to be for you as well, I am resolved to relive my suffering in the hope that you may learn from my mistakes."

He paused, cleared his throat, then continued, "I don't think I ever told you that I was born in Cnidos, a prosperous city in Asia Minor, on the Aegean, and freed by Rome.

"Like your father, mine was the most important producer of wine in the region. His vineyards were so extensive that they not only provided for the local needs but every year enabled him to export wine as far as Athens, Alexandria, and Rome.

"As a child I loved to watch the ships depart for those distant places. I was always the first of my brothers to run down to the port to watch the operations in progress: the carts that arrived piled staggeringly high with crates, the delicate transfer of the amphoras from the pier to the ship, which I watched with bated breath until they disappeared into the hold.

"When the provisions, too, had been loaded and everything was ready, I waited for the first thud of oars hitting water, the maneuvers of the ship as it left the port, and then I stayed to watch as it put out to sea, carried by an invisible force.

"Finally, as it crossed the line of the horizon, I would say to myself, 'Someday I, too, will go to Athens, Alexandria, and Rome.' Alas, I didn't know how unlucky such a prediction would turn out to be! As I've told you, I was only a child, with a dreamy character, spoiled by my mother's attention and used to all the comforts. Following my father's wishes—for he intended eventually to entrust to me the administration of the vineyards—I had at my disposal the best teachers of arithmetic, geometry, and music, to which he gave as much importance as to philosophy.

"When I was fifteen he sent me to Athens to complete my studies. It was my first disappointment.

"Although the city had been rebuilt and beautified by Augustus, Trajan, and Hadrian after the sack of Silla, there was no trace of the marvelous, spirited place I had so often imagined during my readings: on the Acropolis I had the feeling of finding myself not in the real world but, rather, in a vanishing dream of great Rome. In spite of the lively activity of the port, and the numerous schools for the offspring of important families that flourished there, it seemed to me that I was present at a performance that preserved only a faint echo of life.

"The whole city had been reduced to a theater, and our philosophy into material for elegant, enervated discussion. Perhaps it's not easy for you to understand. You only need to know that, at fifteen, I had, for the first time, the sensation of belonging to a world that was already dead. And my dismay was increased by the fact that no one else seemed to notice, that each continued to play his part, great or small, without doubting either its nature or its actual substance.

"Then from Cnidos came the news that an unknown disease had struck the vineyards of the region, including my father's. Experts, wizards, and priests were consulted, who vainly prescribed potions, philters, and expiatory sacrifices. Within a month the vines had withered and the grapes shriveled. Without a harvest, my father wasn't able to pay his debts. The lands were confiscated to repay his creditors and he died of apoplexy the very day they were seized.

"Soon afterward, my mother and my two younger brothers, who had embarked for Samos, where my mother's sister lived, perished at sea, swallowed up by a storm.

"I was eighteen and alone in the world. I soon found myself without a drachma in my pocket. In order not to demean myself by work, I lived on charity. And although the memory of such impiety still shames me, to appease my hunger I often took alms and offerings from the holy altars.

"One morning, as I was wandering around the port scavenging in the mounds of garbage, my sight blurred by starvation, I thought I recognized a slave market.

"It wasn't my mind that made the decision. Even before it

could formulate the slightest thought, my body had gathered its last strength to lead me into the presence of an Egyptian merchant who was busy examining, one after another, women and men, young and old, healthy and infirm. Despite the gravity of the moment, when my turn came I couldn't take my eyes off his sparkling teeth, which shone against his dark skin every time he asked me a question. He inquired about my age, the state of my health, where I came from. He examined hands, teeth, and joints. From my manner of speaking he understood without explanation that I not only knew how to read and write but was well educated.

"In the end, as he handed over the agreed-upon sum in exchange for my freedom, even that Alexandrian used to every sort of commerce let slip a grimace of contempt.

"In the space of a few minutes, my greatest tragedy was consummated.

"It was not birth or the unlucky fate of a lost war that enslaved me but the weakness of my own will. That disgrace, which torments me still, like a hidden ulcer, also made your father uneasy when, after a brief stay in Alexandria, the Egyptian brought me to Rome, and he bought me to be in your service.

"What overcame his initial repugnance was the extent and the value of my scholarship. And even today, in spite of the affection he feels for me, in his eyes I catch the reflection of discomfort, the persistent embarrassment of glimpsing, behind the slave Telifrone, the shadow of a free citizen.

"May fortune always be kind to you, Cecilia! May you never find yourself in a situation to lose the possession you consider most precious! But if through ill fortune that should happen, may the gods give you the strength to preserve and defend it, unlike what I did, adding a new sin to the original guilt."

He was silent and I was in tears. For the first time in my whole life Telifrone held me tight in his arms.

C laudia is pregnant, too, four months, although for now the only ones who have been told are her husband, her father, and her sister.

Yesterday she sent me a letter with the news, and asked me to come see her as soon as possible. And this morning I go, accompanied by Daphne.

A slave comes to the door and leads me through the tablinum, which is crowded with busts of ancestors and their wax masks.

Mine are imposing, but those of Manlius Cornelius Dentatus, so gloomy and so numerous, really frighten me, and I always hurry to my friend's room.

I find her busy spinning wool: evidently, being pregnant hasn't changed her habits in the least. It strikes me, in fact, that pregnancy seems to dignify every aspect of that ancient task.

Claudia looks really well, her face is full and relaxed, and mentally, with a pang of grief, I compare it to my mother's, which is so thin.

She herself claims she has never been in such good health: she hasn't suffered from nausea or stomachaches; her skin shows not a blemish. A sign that it will be a boy, as the doctor confirmed, noting that the fetus is in the right part of the womb. She touches her stomach with a gesture of pride, as if it held the most precious treasure in Rome, while her eyes shine with the knowledge that she is carrying in her womb a future emperor of Rome.

"You know, he is destined to unite at least four hereditary lines," she explains, and she goes on from there into a lengthy, intricate identification of the various patrimonies that will one day belong to her son.

I've been with her for less than an hour and already I'm bored to death. Why did she ask me to come?

There is a moment of silence, and finally, as I'm looking for an excuse to say goodbye, she says, "Cecilia, you're the only one I can ask, because you never stopped studying . . . Whereas I am not very well educated, and besides I have a terrible memory. If our prince returns to Rome, I would be invited to take part in the prayer that the hundred and nine matrons address to Juno the Queen, in the temple of Jove on the Capitoline . . . — you know it?—in the presence of Marcus Aurelius, Commodus, the Praetorian Prefect, and all the other *Quindecemviri*, in addition to the Vestals. Here . . ." and she holds out a parchment.

I take it, and look at Claudia without understanding what she expects from me.

"Even though the Emperor dictates the phrases, it's better to learn it by heart beforehand," she explains. "All I'm asking is that you correct me while I try to repeat it."

I ask her when the prayer is to take place.

"The second of June. They say that the Emperor intends to proclaim Secular Games . . ."

"It's barely September. If you learn it now, by June you will have forgotten it already. And then who knows if Marcus Aurelius will be able to return . . ."

"But yes: just last night, after I prayed for him, he appeared to me in a dream, in a triumphal chariot, along with Commodus . . . The message is clear: our prince will soon defeat the barbarians and return to Rome."

She insists that she has to start practicing right away, otherwise she'll never make it. She begs me in any case to help her.

How can I refuse? Why not take the opportunity to show that for once, at least, I can be affectionate and patient?

And so the torture begins.

Sometimes pompously, sometimes stammering, skipping half the words, starting from the beginning every time, Claudia begins to declaim the following formula:

"Queen Juno, if fortune can be even more propitious for the citizens of Rome, Let us entreat and implore you. Let us, the hundred and nine mothers of families of the citizens of Rome, all married, beseech you to increase the power and sovereignty of the citizens of Rome, at home and abroad, to grant eternal protection, victory, and strength to the citizens of Rome, to sustain the citizens of Rome and their legions, to keep safe and sound the republic of the citizens of Rome, to extend it further, and to be kind to the citizens of Rome, to the *Quindecemviri*, to us, our houses, our families. This is why we entreat you, invoke you, and implore you, we, mothers of families of the citizens of Rome, all married, all kneeling."

While my friend struggles to respect every pause, to find the right tone, I wonder how in the world Juno can welcome a prayer that's so badly written, a prayer so dry, boring, and repetitious. Learning it by heart is quite an undertaking, because all the sentences have almost the same meaning, and so there is no reason that one should come before or after another. I also wonder how our philosopher prince, although respectful of every ritual, can stand such nonsense.

I am on the point of saying to Claudia that she's taking the thing too seriously, but when I see her so anxious to prove herself worthy of being numbered among the hundred and nine matrons all married, all kneeling, learning perfectly those dead words, I don't have the courage.

I don't want to see anyone, I don't want to hear anything, all I want is to withdraw into myself in the hope of finding some peace.

"Be indifferent in joy as in sorrow. Accept willingly everything that happens, even if it causes suffering, because it leads beyond, to the health of the cosmos, to the happy and successful outcome of Jove's design."

No, I have too many criticisms to bring against him and his triumph, which seems yet again to be fulfilled to the detriment of our existence. I would like to look Pallante in the eye and say, "Yes, I am so wicked I will complain about the gods. I will break all the vows, which they ignore anyway. Just as they ignore prayers and libations. The gods don't care about us. And I have never cared about improving myself."

Yesterday's events were so painful that I long for the tedium of the time I spent with Claudia.

My brother decided not to enter life.

Lucilla miscarried again.

From my room I heard her cry out. She called Mirrina, she called my father, even though she knew that he wouldn't be home at that hour.

I ran to her, even before her maid, and found her writhing in her bed, screaming and sobbing. The blood gushed as if from a poisonous fountain, soaking her tunic, staining the covers and the mattress.

As I stared at the dark stains, with no idea of how to help, Mirrina arrived, stopped for a second at the bed, and hurried off. My mother turned on me an imploring gaze, then began to scream again, tightening her hands around her stomach, as if to hold on to her child.

"Tell me what to do," I stammered.

She didn't answer, maybe she didn't even hear me, so I went in search of help. At the door I ran into Mirrina, who was carrying a basin of hot water, followed by Carite with a pile of towels in her arms.

Every attempt to approach her to stem the bleeding or dry her sweaty forehead was vain, because she wouldn't stop thrashing and kicking, ordering them to go away, to leave her child in peace.

I was about to start sobbing, but Carite noticed and sent me to tell Milone to get my father immediately.

When he arrived, the child had vanished, liquefied in a black river, reduced to clots of blood scattered on the bed.

They changed the mattress and covers, washed Lucilla; my father gave her an infusion to drink, and she fell asleep.

I can't erase the image of all that black blood or last night's bad dream. Now I remember my first menstruation, when I was thirteen.

Then, too, the blood began to gush early in the morning, staining my tunic, the insides of my thighs, and the bed.

Of a bright, almost transparent red, it flowed without causing me the slightest pain. But if its appearance left me indifferent, it brought joy to my parents, worried that the puberty of their only daughter was so slow in arriving.

So, without even telling Carite, without taking care to wash or change my tunic, I wrapped a towel around my waist and hurried to bring the news to Lucilla.

By the time I got to her room, the blood was dripping on the floor and on my feet. And while she, uncomprehending, insisted on knowing where I was wounded, I, in a distorted vision that made me blind and deaf to everything around me, for the first time saw Quintus's body, still bloody, superimposed on mine. While she stripped me to make sure of what had happened and sent for Carite, while my nurse took off my tunic and scrubbed my legs and feet, for all that time, completely inert, a doll in their hands, I again felt overwhelmed by the immensity of my sin.

Quintus was bitten by a snake because I broke our pact. Refusing to pay the penalty and walk on the nettles, I challenged what was sacred. And he died to make amends for my profanation when, really, Dis was waiting for me. With an act of pridefulness I exchanged my destiny with his, removed myself from the plan of Fate, carrying out the most serious crime: leading an innocent to ruin.

A certainty that last night made the dream of my bloody friend even more cruel. A terrible vision, one of the ones I never revealed to anyone before writing it on these papyruses, and whose ferocity subsides only when I talk to you, Annia, sure of your love.

For three days I've hardly seen my father at all. I need him, and his comfort, and maybe I could even console him. Instead he hasn't a moment for me, he's always taken up by his obligations, looking increasingly sad and oppressed. I remember better times, when he was a doctor, and the house wasn't invaded from early morning by that nagging throng, all asking something from Paulus, all insincere and opportunistic . . . Just because he is Prefect of the Annona.

I'm sad that my mother miscarried, but I'm angry with her. It's her fault if our life has changed for the worse.

After the famous quarrel six years ago between Lucilla and Uncle Julius, I seem to see them again, my father and mother, discussing endlessly.

At the table, she talks on and on about her father's will; the reading was finally held. Julius wrote to her that, apart from insulting him, calling him weak and a spendthrift, grandfather disinherited him in favor of Aulus, whereas his sister's part was left intact. He warns her, though, that, since he has made a decision to contest the will, things will drag on for her, too. Giving the impression of taking up a subject that has arisen before, Lucilla says obstinately that when the moment arrives nothing in the world will make her accept a guardian. My father tries to point out that the law now allows her to choose one at her pleasure, and, besides, it's widely known that those administrators will go along with the wishes of their clients.

But for her it's a matter of principle: only an evil fate deprived her of the three children necessary to have free access to what is owed her by law. She tried in every way to respect the law, to give Rome its Quirites. Perhaps unique among her friends, she challenged the risks of pregnancy and birth, put her own life in jeopardy many times, not to mention the disfigurement of her body, the premature aging.

She wants her petition to go as high as the emperor if necessary: she is claiming an exception to the law, asking that both her misfortune and her good will be recognized. She knows of other matrons who have succeeded in that same purpose.

But one must be in a position to give and receive favors and protection, have the right friends. And Paulus, too occupied with his patients, his studies, the management of his lands, has failed to cultivate them. It's time for him to enter public service, the only way to guarantee that esteem which the practice of medicine has up to now obscured. After all, his father was a member of the equestrian order, and, although he's been dead for some time, his reputation has not faded.

Yes, it seems to me that I hear the energy with which Lucilla asserts her convictions! And my father, who answers cautiously, and, to indulge her a little, names some of his patients of especially elevated rank, who might perhaps help him. He also mentions Galen, Marcus Aurelius's doctor, but ever since he took the liberty of rebuking him for his contemptuous manner and his overly polemical attitude toward other doctors, their friendship has somewhat cooled.

Then finally he rouses himself: no, it's not the moment to think about such changes. The wine trade is worsening from year to year. Alcimus, who has always seen to it, is no longer able to compete with the production that is flooding Italy from the provinces.

Just now he himself went over the accounts with the

farmer. Because of the breeding of slaves, costs are rising precipitously. They can't go on like that, there is the danger of ruin.

Measures must be taken: at any rate, he has summoned Alcimus, in order to come to a decision.

Ah, if only things had gone like that, if my father had continued to oppose her!

But in the end he does what Lucilla asks. Long past thirty, he abandons his beloved practice of the art of medicine, which he learned from the slave Alexandros in his father's house, and devotes himself both to the transformation of his patrimonial lands and to the pursuit of a public career.

We return to Rome from Umbria in late autumn, when the fear of infection is dormant.

Little by little I learn that my father has sold a part of the Umbrian property to acquire other property in Sicily, and that the majority of the vineyards—apart from those in the Tiber valley that produce a renowned wine—have been returned to pasture and grain.

He builds mills and ovens for bread, arranges apprenticeships for the slaves. He has marble quarries dug in the property near Carrara that constitutes my mother's dowry, and sulfur mines in Sicily.

Every day I rush to say good morning, but every day, as now, I'm disappointed. The door of his doctor's office now locked forever, he goes out before dawn to visit friends or the children of friends of his father or of my maternal grandfather or some former patient who is a senator—anyone who might be able to help him on the path to public office.

When I ask Lucilla about him she explains that he has finally decided to win that position which was ordained for him by birth, rectitude, and wealth.

At home I've never seen so many new faces, nor have so many banquets been given, and so lavish.

One name, in particular, recurs continuously in the conversations of my parents, that of the prefect Gaius Publius Primus, a man of vast fortune, and very respected at court, who has taken Paulus's situation to heart.

Meanwhile, a new teacher, chosen personally by Lucilla, is engaged for me, Drusus. Thanks to my mother and my pedagogue, I know how to read and write both Greek and Latin correctly. I can therefore move on to the study of grammar and commentary on the great poets.

And now Drusus comes every morning, draped in a cloak that accentuates the severity of his bearing.

He makes me repeat till I'm exhausted the six cases of the noun and the twenty-seven classes into which common nouns are subdivided, even when it's obvious that I already know them by heart; conjugate the same irregular verb a hundred times; list for hours the prepositions and the cases they govern. (At least you were spared these tortures, Annia!)

Although my tutor has absolutely none of Domitian's malice, although his rigidity is combined with tremendous patience, after the freedom I've had I feel imprisoned again in a barren, inhospitable land.

I seldom see Telifrone and Carite, and I miss my parents, who are constantly busy, receiving guests or taking part in engagement celebrations and weddings, public readings and shows at the arena or the theater.

Besides, great renovations are taking place in the empty house, which echoes all day with the hammers of sculptors and carpenters, the coming and going of painters and mosaicists. Sometimes the uproar is so great that even Drusus has trouble concentrating.

One morning he is reading the last lines of the second book of the *Georgics*, on the happy lives of farmers, who, ignorant of luxury and the deceits of power, live in peace. Suddenly he is interrupted by a huge crash, maybe a block of marble falling.

When the last cry of alarm in the house has faded, Drusus says only, "Precisely."

I don't know what deceits may await my father in his new life, but in the end, thanks to the protection of Gaius Publius Primus and his network of acquaintances, Paulus receives the gold ring of the equestrian order and a position as procurator. And when, later, in the atrium, adorned with statues and new frescoes, a line of clients begins to file by, a line that gets longer every morning, my mother can receive her paternal inheritance and dispose of it without being subject to a guardian.

And yet, far from placating her, reaching her goal seems to have exacerbated a sense of defeat, as if seeing her good will as mother and matron publicly recognized made the loss of her children even more unbearable.

Little by little the energy she put into the construction of her husband's career diminishes, and she begins to wander aimlessly again, like a grindstone without grain, feeding on the old sadness.

Who, Lucilla, benefited from all this upheaval?

Nothing seems changed from the days when she was pregnant.

My mother continues to spend all her time in bed, and the house is still sunk in silence. But it's a different silence, which seems to contain the echo of the marble slab closing the sarcophagus forever.

And yet I call myself fortunate, I call our parents fortunate, because that brother was only a dream, not a child in flesh and blood like you, Annia, or Flavius.

For a long time our mother went on talking about him, the brother we didn't know. Of how lively and obedient he was, how affectionate and intelligent. Of his eyes and his black hair, and how much he looked like her.

She spoke of him as if he were still alive, then halfway through a sentence she would stop, and was mute for days.

When, as a child, I burst into her room, a veil of disappointment dimmed her gaze: maybe, in her preoccupation, the sound of my running feet had abolished time, announcing not my arrival but that of her favorite child.

I felt her lips cold on my cheek and wished I could disappear. But that would have taken a magic spell, because I would never be strong enough to leave her.

Only later, Annia, with your first steps, when you could come with me to her room, only then that desire to vanish was appeased. Being two protected me, divided the impact of her gaze, softened the rejection.

When Daphne announced that Pallante had arrived, I had her say that I had a stomachache and couldn't see him. Anyway I've decided: I'll tell my father that I don't want him to be my teacher anymore.

If—as all he does is repeat to me—the present is the only good available to us, it doesn't seem right to waste it in exercises that, at least on me, have even less effect than physical ones, which they resemble.

I prefer to talk about virtue with Drusus, who, behind a hair-splitting rigidity and a sometimes brutal severity, shows a respect, a more genuine and sincere search for the truth. Even from Telifrone's noble despair I could learn more.

And I prefer by far poetry, music, and singing—when a fragment of eternity descends on me—to the arid discipline imposed by philosophy.

I don't know what arguments my father used to persuade Lucilla to get up, to have her hair washed by Mirrina, to take off the tunic that since the day of the miscarriage she had refused to change, to put on a clean and elegant one for the occasion of yesterday's dinner.

But sitting on the couch of honor, between my father and Ennius Severus, the Prefect of Grain Distribution, she didn't say a word during the entire evening.

Neither did Lucretia, next to me and Carvilius Ruga, or Pallante, who, on a couch of his own, seemed to be carefully making a show of the indifference with which he tasted every dish.

The liveliest dialogue took place on the couch on the right, occupied by Junia Decidiana, her new husband, Minicius Acilianus, and the poet Seleucus, who is always ready to declaim his own verses and comment on them with the other guests.

Suddenly Carvilius intervened in the poetic jousting, reciting epigrams of Martial to illustrate the food as it was served.

In front of a basket of mushrooms, he exclaimed with satisfaction, "Silver, gold, a cloak, a toga are easy gifts to send; what's hard to send is mushrooms."

Tasting a truffle: "We truffles, who with tender head break the nourishing earth, are the fruit of the earth, second only to mushrooms."

From the way Carvilius looked around after reciting each poem, it was clear that he expected a sign of appreciation. And so the guests began to clap, except for my mother, Lucretia, and Pallante, whose gaze traveled a span above the heads of the other guests.

"No matter how big the plate that holds the turbot, the turbot is always bigger than the plate."

How accurate, what a memory, bravo Carvilius, hooray!

A deadly bore, that banquet. An idiotic display. I observed my father, who was smiling with a tolerant air. Who knows what goes through his head? Is he really amused? How is it possible? Then I looked at poor Lucretia, who, pale as a corpse, had not touched any food.

I took advantage of a moment of confusion to ask if she didn't feel well.

"It's torture, Cecilia," she whispered in my ear. "Aurelius doesn't come around anymore, doesn't answer my letters—he's disappeared. Sometimes I'm afraid he's dead; sometimes I'm sure he's betrayed me, and pray Jove to strike him with a thunderbolt. May I come and see you tomorrow? I desperately need to talk to you."

I told her that of course I would expect her.

As a cupbearer with honey-colored eyes poured his wine Carvilius resumed his citations, casting obscene glances at the boy: "Attic honey, you thicken the nectar-like Falernian: it's a drink that's worthy of being mixed by Ganymede."

This time no one congratulated him: that Carvilius, at his age, not only still cultivates a taste for boys but doesn't even take the trouble to hide it is judged utterly inappropriate. There was a silence that he hurried to fill, reciting at random: "Great Verona owes its Catullus as much as small Mantua its Virgil."

Another silence, this time of bewilderment. Seleucus, who has an ear for the slightest danger of discord at a banquet, and a great fear of not being invited back, tried to remedy the embarrassing situation by declaiming with vacuous appropriateness:

First, if life remains I will return to my homeland,
bringing the Muses with me, led from the Aonian peak;
first, o Mantua, I will bring back to you the palms of
Idumaea . . .

Carvilius sighed with relief, and everyone applauded. Then, proudly, Ennius Severus said that the Emperor in person had written to inform him about the new phases of peace-making in Germany, and while Minicius Acilianus looked at him in admiration, slightly envious, the prefect invited everyone to toast the health and glory of Caesar.

There was a moment of silence, to which even Pallante, closing his eyes, was willing to lend the intensity of his thoughts, followed by a discussion of the negotiations with the Quadi, the Marcomanni, and the Iazyges.

"To settle matters quickly we'd need another miracle of the rains—along with hail and lightning that would strike the barbarians but spare our men," Seleucus said.

"Have you heard the latest? The Christians, those blowhard atheists, have spread the rumor that the miracle is due to the prayers of their soldiers," Minicius added, with a laugh. But no one, it seemed, found the news amusing, because the diners again fell silent.

I continued to observe my mother.

Like Lucretia, she had not touched any food.

Most of the time she stared straight ahead.

Only from time to time, at regular intervals and in an almost mechanical way, she turned her head toward the guest of honor, nodding if he spoke to her.

Then my father asked me to play for the guests. Daphne brought the zither and I sat on a stool in the middle of the room.

To tell the truth I felt slightly embarrassed. But gradually, as the notes filled the room, I forgot all those eyes on me, even the

sharp gaze of Ennius Severus. I forgot the tedium of the dinner, the foolish displays of the men, all the sadness of the
women, of my mother and Lucretia, and my longing for your
company, Annia, you who would have cheered it. And when
the conversation began again, I was so absorbed in the music
that I no longer noticed anything. Only for a moment, turning
to look at the table, I noticed that Junia had left her place and
was now talking into Lucilla's ear.

Today my mother again refused to leave her bed.

To keep her company I offer to read from the *Thebaid* of Statius. Personally I find the poem insipid, with not very interesting characters, but I hope that all those descriptions of marvelous divine interventions might distract her. She keeps her eyes closed, but as soon as I stop and anxiously scrutinize her, she says, "Please, continue, and don't look at me like that."

So I start reading again, but I can't seem to concentrate on the words.

Then Junia arrives; these days she's always wearing the same white linen tunic with a black fringed shawl knotted under her breast. She has a serious, absorbed look, as if she were keeping who knows what secret. And in fact, after a few hurried questions about my mother's health, she sits down on the edge of the bed and begins, "Lucilla, you know how fond I am of you— because we're cousins, because we spent so many years together as children . . . I can sense your slightest change of mood, even before it shows. And now I feel your suffering, I really feel as if this dead child were mine. I never told you, but for a while I've been going to the temple of the goddess Isis . . ."

My mother, who has been listening with her eyes closed, opens them, looking at her with an expression both amazed and mocking. But Junia, who really does know her well, raises a hand to stop her from speaking.

"I know what you think. That I am the usual dupe. I know you're surprised. And how can I hope to persuade you to follow me to a place that to many, excited by prejudice, is merely a cradle of lust and superstition? But it's not like that. Please, let me tell you the story of the goddess . . ."

My mother says nothing and Junia continues, "The story is that Isis was the sister of Osiris, and the two were so in love that they united in the darkness of their mother's womb. She so loved Osiris, her brother-spouse, that when Typhon had him treacherously shut up in an ark and abandoned at the mouth of the river, she cut off one of her tresses and put on robes of mourning. From that day she wandered aimlessly, not knowing where to look, asking everyone she met for news of the ark; she asked even children about it. When, finally, she found it, she opened it immediately, fell on Osiris, and began to kiss him, weeping. Then she placed the ark in a hiding place, but Typhon discovered it and, recognizing the body of Osiris, cut it into fourteen pieces and scattered them. When Isis found out she began searching again, crossing swamps on a raft made of papyrus, and for every piece she recovered she built a tomb. Out of devotion, of course, but also because in this way Typhon, confronted by such disparate evidence, would never find the true tomb. Isis demonstrated the same great love toward her son Horus, conceived by uniting with Osiris after his death. This probably all seems to you a fantastic invention, but the pilgrimage of Isis in search of her brother-spouse, all the difficulties and struggles she faced, the proof she gives of wisdom and courage, make her the goddess closest to our women's hearts. Come to the temple with me, come and ask for her help, so that, in her compassion, in her tenderness, she may end your grief and bring you peace and repose."

Junia is silent, and although the story she has just finished must appear to Lucilla, too, quite extraordinary, as well as rather confused, I realized that she hadn't missed a word. She is about to answer when Daphne arrives to tell me that Lucretia is waiting in my room.

"I haven't finished hearing sad stories," I say to myself, crossing the garden to join her.

And in fact here's my friend, with her hair loose and in disarray, and her face streaked with tears. Beside her, Acme seems to shine with newfound pleasures of love. Quickly, repeatedly, I glance from one to the other, until my old suspicion of the maid becomes conviction: it's with her that Aurelius has always betrayed Lucretia! And she's so brazen that she holds her head high all the while her mistress is giving voice to her torment, sure that he's abandoned her for someone else. There's no other explanation for that disappearance, the silence with which he responds to her letters.

She tortures herself trying to figure out who this woman could be: she gets lost in a thousand conjectures, thinking back over every situation—at the theater, the arena, at a banquet—where she and her lover have been together, certain that the betrayal began in her presence. Was there perhaps someone who, if fleetingly, roused his interest? A particularly attractive girl? Does she recall having noticed in Aurelius a gesture, a look, a sudden change of mood? No, she remembers nothing. But maybe she doesn't remember well: she has to struggle, begin at the beginning, re-examine every situation in its smallest details.

Halfway through yet another examination, she is struck by the opposite certainty, and that is that Aurelius's new lover is a woman she has never seen.

What's her name? Where could Aurelius have met her? Is she fair? Or dark, like her? Taller, shorter? A married woman, a slave, a courtesan?

She will kill her. Rather, she'll kill them both, wretched despicable people, the bastard, the whore! She'll dig out their hearts, damn them to eternity!

Exhausted, she feels that she's experiencing death, although she is still alive. She no longer has eyes to see, ears to hear, she feels she has lost everything, the whole world, now that she has lost him. An emptiness, an immense weariness invades her. She throws herself on her bed, begging Morpheus to welcome her into his arms. But soon in a dream the cruel god delivers her into the arms of Aurelius, returning to delude her with the ecstasies of love. Every waking renews her grief, revives the wound: what a fool she was to leave him alone so many nights! How she regrets wanting to hide her own ardor! Yes, of course, it is all her fault if in the end Aurelius preferred another. Lucretia lists her own sins, and each contradicts the other: she never let him know how much she loved him, she made her love too easy for him, she was too aloof and too yielding, too sad and too happy, too careless in her dress and too elegant.

Every so often as my friend describes her sufferings I glance at Acme. What should I do? Wouldn't it be right to reveal the deception? But will knowing make her feel better? Or will it increase her pain? And what if she reacts the way she did when I tried to expose her lover with Ovid's verses?

In the end I tell her the most banal thing in the world, and that is that Aurelius doesn't deserve her.

"Yes, I know you've always thought that, and you've always wanted to put me on my guard. But the truth is, Cecilia, that you don't know him: he's the kindest man, the best creature in the world. He loves me, and I'm sure he'll come back."

nnia, amid a thousand doubts and torments, I'll try to write what Daphne just told me.

In an outburst of anger at her mistress, Mirrina let slip that a short time after your death Lucilla had a lover, Marcus, a young slave our father had just brought to the house.

Apparently she felt for him the sort of adoration and affection that are usually reserved for a god or a small child. She overwhelmed him with attentions and gifts and, without the least shame, under all eyes, received him in her room even during the day. She didn't care about hiding it from her husband. Once, he found her on her knees in front of the slaves' rooms, and Lucilla confessed that she was in agony because Marcus was late coming home. Amid her tears she said wicked, crazy things: once she had been someone, then she was nothing, until that boy gave her new life. As if the same blood ran in their veins: the only other creature she had felt that close to was her son Flavius, whom Marcus's tenderness and gaiety reminded her of.

Without a word, our father helped her up, led her to her room, and stayed with her until her tears stopped. For months he pretended not to notice anything. When, finally, his wife's ardor seemed to have lessened, he sold Marcus to an acquaintance.

Convinced that she was doing me a favor, and ignorant of the pain she was causing, Daphne didn't omit a detail of Mirrina's story. And now my mind is in turmoil: I feel sorry for

Lucilla and angry at her, and the same toward our father. One moment she seems arrogant, shameless, and dishonest (she who wanted to destroy the papyruses because they recounted Lucretia's love for Aurelius). He, weak and cowardly. The next moment, Lucilla's folly grieves me, while I see in Paulus the gentlest and most affectionate man in the world. Where will they ever find a husband who loves me the way he loves his wife! Dear sister, my trembling fingers can't hold the pen any longer. I have to put it down, leave the room: but a hundred laps around the garden will not be enough to calm me. I would have to run thousands and thousands of miles.

W hat sort of friend would I be if I didn't prove to be honest? If, possessing a truth so important for her, I had kept it to myself, betraying her trust and abandoning her to deception?

So, after reflecting for a long time, weighing the pros and cons, yesterday I went to see Lucretia to tell her about my suspicions.

Naturally I already regret it, but even more, and for different reasons, than the time when I wrote to warn her.

In fact, at the moment itself she reacted with surprising calm. She thanked me for my loyalty, for having driven out any trace of illusion. With unusual understanding, in an almost philosophical tone, she said that ultimately the truth, however painful, always has a healing power on the soul.

Then she summoned Acme.

She looked at her for a moment without saying a word, examining the lovely oval of her face, her shining black eyes, her full lips, and then, suddenly, she hurled herself at her. She scratched her face and beat her. Then, grabbing her by the hair, she threw her to the floor and punched and kicked her.

I witnessed that havoc, paralyzed by opposing impulses. Every time I made a move to stop her, something arrested me, and again I stared at my friend raging like a Fury at her maid. I don't know how much time passed before the knowledge that she would kill her got through to me, but suddenly I see myself grabbing her hips, tugging her hard, with all my strength, to separate her from her victim.

Lucretia stood staring at her while the poor girl writhed, groaning, her face swollen and bloody. Then, still panting, she said, "I'm not going to kill you, because I would be the one to pay. But with the statements I will make against you there is not a Roman who will buy you. You will end up in a brothel, which after all is the place you deserve. And don't dare gossip about it. I will accuse you of theft, and I have enough important friends to send you to forced labor."

Annia, I'll tell you in a whisper, because I'm ashamed: I was still trembling, and yet in a hidden corner my soul rejoiced.

My mother is getting better. She's still pale, but it's a different pallor, the result of an internal tension, a new concentration.

Some time after telling her the story of Isis and Osiris, Junia persuaded her to go with her to the temple of the Egyptian goddess in the Campus Martius. And ever since Lucilla has been there every day.

Yesterday, when I went to say good morning, she was preparing to return.

"You know, Cecilia," she said to me, in a voice full of expectation, which I hadn't heard for a long time, "neither I nor your father cares about the opinions of others, the gossip that will inevitably spread about the wife of the Prefect of the Annona, who goes to places of vice. But he disapproves, maintaining that this belief only inflames sensibility and exaggerates thoughts. He finds those women who in penitence bathe in the frigid Tiber and then drag themselves naked through the streets with bloodied knees indecent, theatrical, and, finally, ridiculous. I, too, thought the same thing at first, because I didn't understand the true nature of the worship of Isis, but now that I know it better I realize that she is the dispenser of wisdom, the source of purity and profound consolation."

I chased away the image of Lucilla kneeling at her lover's door and coldly asked her how the Egyptian worship was different from that of our divinities.

"It is closer to me," she answered, pushing away the hand of Mirrina, who was spreading ceruse on her forehead.

"As my cousin explained, Isis understands the suffering of women because she experienced it. Although she is a goddess, she knows evil and death, the loss of a beloved creature. But she also knows hope and rebirth. I'll tell you the extraordinary dream I had last night, because it will illuminate her nature for you. After a violent shipwreck, in which all of you died, I found myself alone on a beach. My eyes filled with tears, I scanned the horizon, praying to the gods to restore to me at least one of you, when Isis herself emerged from the waves, wrapped in a black cloak and shining with a dark light. In that light, giving off a fragrance of Arabian essences, she deigned to address these words to me: 'Here I am for you, Lucilla, moved by your prayers. I, the mother of all things, mistress of all the elements, beginning of all the generations through the centuries, the greatest of the divinities. Here I am for you, touched by your misfortunes, here I am for you, kind and propitious. Abandon your weeping and laments, banish sorrow: thanks to me, the day of salvation already shines for you. And so listen carefully to my command. The day that is about to arise from this night, and the next two, are sacred to my worship. Go to this celebration, and let your mind not be distracted or profane.'"

My mother broke off, sighed, then added, solemnly, "So the goddess spoke, and I awoke, filled with fear and joy, unable to sleep again, I was so anxious to carry out her orders and go to the celebration. But, Cecilia, I would like you to come with me. I want you, too, to see and understand."

So I accompanied her to the celebration of Isis, and was so shaken that I despair of finding the words to express the sorrow and elation, the aura of madness and, at the same time, extraordinary mystery surrounding the rite.

When we got to the Campus Martius the procession was already winding from the temple toward the Tiber.

In front was a group of women dressed in white who were scattering flowers on the streets. A huge crowd followed, with lanterns, torches, and candles, and meanwhile a chorus of children began singing a hymn, while flutists and bagpipers devoted to the Egyptian god played a poignant melody. Last came the heralds, shouting to clear the way for the sacred procession.

And in fact the initiates into the mysteries of Isis were arriving, men and women of every station and age—the women wearing a transparent veil over their heads, the men completely shaved, skulls bare—who jingled sistrums of bronze, silver, and gold. After them came the high priests, in white linen tunics, each bearing an emblem of the gods.

But what struck me most in this procession was the common women, the simple worshippers.

They were like a river that in its course breaks off into a thousand streams, as every so often one of them detached herself from the group to act out Isis's search for the beloved remains of Osiris. Beating her breast amid cries and laments, she would run in one direction and then another, asking now this one, now that if he had seen the mutilated body of her brother-spouse, as she searched in a bush or in the shade of a tree, calling his name.

My mother, who walked beside me and Mirrina, observed them almost timidly at first.

Suddenly, however, infected by their ardor, or perhaps remembering the goddess's command, she moved away from us and began to imitate them. She, too, beat her breast in a sign of mourning, and I understood that she was weeping for the death of each of her children, yours, Annia, and that of Flavius and the other, nameless ones. She relived the pain of each premature death, then, invoking Osiris, she expressed the desire for all of you to be reborn into a new life.

Confused by the crowd, the shouts, and the laments, moved and yet frightened, I watched Lucilla. Never had I so feared, distrusted, and at the same time hoped.

Miraculously freed from every resentment toward her, I hoped that Isis would heal the pain that neither a foolish, disgraceful love nor the attainment of high offices and honors had been able to make up for or hide.

I hoped that Isis would restore her children to her, and that you, Annia, would be restored to me, thanks to the future life that she was ready to grant you. It seemed to me that I understood the intimate, almost familial power of the goddess who had known death. It seemed to me that I could believe, and not only imagine, that you really hear my words.

Then I was afraid that Lucilla would lose her reason, that her mind would go to pieces like the body of the Egyptian god. In her frenetic gestures I recognized the persistence of her illness. I thought of our father, I thought of Pallante and Drusus. I saw them shaking their heads, their worried, cold, and mocking gaze, and suddenly, like them, I felt repulsion and contempt for the great mother with the bovine horns, for the worshippers shouting like bad actresses on a stage. Again I was hit by a violent wave of resentment.

As the clanging of the sistrums cut through the wailing of flutes and bagpipes, and my mother continued to get lost in the crowd and return, beginning her search anew each time, we, too, reached the river.

Some women had already gone down, each to a different boat. And each held in her hand a rope, tied to a second boat containing a chest on which the figure of a black-winged bird was painted. While the joyful cries of the faithful resounded from the bank, the women pulled the boat toward themselves, rejoicing that they had found the body of Osiris.

But when her turn came Lucilla refused to get in the boat. She stammered that she wasn't yet ready for such a great hope, she didn't yet feel that she was deserving or strong enough to sustain it, and that the goddess would understand.

Then, leaning on me and Mirrina, she moved aside to leave room for the woman who came after her. She said that she needed air, and walking silently along the river, we headed home.

PART TWO

L ast night I fell asleep with the window open, and when I woke the blue winter sky, high and bright, seemed to arc above me without offering any shelter, magnifying the emptiness and silence that reign in my new house.

In all that silence I remembered the papyruses, and their subtle feel, and I looked for them in the few chests that haven't been opened. I was afraid I had lost or maybe destroyed them, judging them foolish, or in an impulse of anger and despair that I no longer remembered.

Instead they appeared, a bit crumpled, in a pile of scrolls. It seemed to me I had not touched them since my first meeting with Valerian, and reading them again made an extraordinary impression. Barely recognizing my own writing, I read some lines at random without remembering that I had written them. The events recounted seemed novel, and even the girl who said her name was Cecilia seemed unknown to me.

And now? What should I record now on this blank sheet? I look for the voice that spoke to you, Annia, but I no longer hear it.

If I am no longer the same Cecilia, the room I am in is different, too, the light that filters through a small high window, and the bed, which is not that of my childhood.

Yesterday Valerian left Rome to visit his property in Campania, without saying when he will return. We've been married for two months, and yet I already know he is so mysterious that any length of time is a challenge.

C arite warned me.

She had heard them the night before, the master and mistress, talking about the Prefect of Grain Distribution and his son Valerian. My mother insisted that it should be done quickly, for soon I would be sixteen, and they could not wait a day longer for me to prepare to bring an heir into the world. My father cheered her with good news of the progress in the negotiations with Ennius Severus, from whom he had learned that Valerian, among the first to benefit from the new law, had been able to inherit from his mother. If one considered the inheritance he would receive on the death of the prefect, it was therefore an even better match than he had thought. Further, Ennius Severus had agreed to insert a clause that forbade the future husband from taking a concubine. He had only to decide on the dowry, but since he intended to be generous he was sure that the agreement would soon be concluded. Then he had said, sighing, that although he had been preparing for this separation for years, now that it was close he knew that he would never be ready to live far from his daughter.

Then my nurse had announced, "Child, the great moment has arrived! Get ready to meet your future husband."

For two more days during the celebration of Isis, I had seen Lucilla, dressed in white linen, leave before dawn to go to the temple and replay the sacred pantomime of mourning and the resurrection of her children. Two nights I had seen her return, distraught and luminous, absent and rapt. Right in that period my father was away, occupied by a serious emergency: it was said that a storm had destroyed at least three ships, and the grain was late in arriving from Africa.

So on the third day, when Carite reported their nocturnal council, I wondered with what residual power or attention, in what corner of their minds, they had been able to devote a single thought to me.

What a fool I had been. How presumptuous, with my conviction that the gods had given me the gift of extraordinary senses, and that I missed nothing that was happening around me! And yet I who feared marriage more than the plague, who analyzed every word, gesture, and silence of my parents, had not been aware of the plot they were hatching.

I recalled the attentive look that Ennius Severus had given me on the night of the banquet and, even earlier, at the Port, but I had pushed it aside without giving it any weight. Why?

To avoid the anxiety that accompanies all anticipation?

No, I'm not so smart. Then out of laziness, or because, unexpectedly, Pallante's teachings had not been in vain, and I had begun to distinguish the things that depended on me from those enslaved by nature.

When the day came for the meeting with my future fiancé, I repeated to myself, on the way to the tablinum, where my father usually attended to important business, "In the end, it's only this, important business that, sooner or later, had to be attended to."

I remember the strange calm with which this phrase echoed in my mind, as if, reconciling me to destiny, it were delivering my soul to a peace and freedom unknown until now.

On the other hand, I don't know how it was swept away when, as I entered the study, Valerian turned to me—and by the will of Cytherian Venus had neither wrinkles like Carvilius nor a disdainful grimace like Manlius Cornelius Dentatus but a drop of pure light in his eyes—and time seemed to explode, then disappear, shattering the chain of causes and effects, subverting in a single moment all the arrangements of Fate.

In the same way, although I heard it, I remember nothing of the conversation that took place later between Ennius Severus and my parents. From time to time they asked us a question, which Valerian and I answered in monosyllables, heads lowered, each taking care not to meet the other's gaze.

Later, not wanting to talk to anyone, I shut myself in my room and took the papyruses from their hiding place.

"Dear Annia, finally what I feared most in the world has happened. In fact, the complete opposite happened. In a single moment . . . How is it possible? For this moment alone I was born . . ."

I read those few lines again, then I tore the sheet into a thousand pieces.

My daughter, I think that you will be content.

He's only ten years older than you and is still a handsome young man. It's said that he is powerful and has an enterprising spirit, but also great reserve, which will make the respect and obedience that you owe him easier and more natural. He has the reputation of being a brilliant speaker and, since he's already one of the *vigintiviri* and will soon become questor, it's clear that he's working his way up quickly. Furthermore, he's wealthy, and destined to become even more so.

Cecilia, I bet you're already in love, but don't rush, don't become too passionate. No matter how great a man may appear, he's never worth as much as a woman (although in Rome everyone thinks, or pretends to think, the opposite). Also your friend Domitilla has some important and somewhat unexpected news for you, and will come and see you soon. Farewell.

Child, I saw your fiancé, while he was crossing the atrium with his father. His bearing is so noble he already seems a senator!

I was somewhat worried because Milone, who knows a servant of Ennius Severus, had reported to me that Valerian was a real instigator: always the first at night to break down the door of a prostitute, or to thrash an unlucky passerby, always the first to pick a quarrel with the supporters of the White faction. I meant to consult the astrologer Zeusippus, but it was enough to see him to understand that it's all water under the bridge: he's settled down and will be an affectionate and devoted husband for my little Cecilia.

You will take me to your new house, won't you, Cecilia? So that I can teach Homer to your children, as I did to you.

Dear Cecilia, I'm dying to know what your future husband is like . . . There are so many rumors about him, and very different. But luckily it seems that he does not resemble my Carvilius in the least. Answer right away and tell me all the details.

Then it was my father's turn.
"So, my little lady?"
I blushed, incapable of responding.
"You don't want to tell me what you think of Valerian?"
I was silent.
"Is there something you don't like about him?"
How could I say "I like him very much!," hearing in my mind the words of that so-and-so: "If a woman dares to say she is in love one should run from her in horror, rather than take such impudence as the basis for marriage." So I remained mute.
"If you have doubts, if you think you need to see him again, to speak to him more . . . In short, Cecilia, say something."
"No, I don't want to see him again . . ."
"You know that although your refusal would grieve me, I would bear it in mind."
"For me the most important thing is to please you and respect your will," I lied, to get out of this embarrassment.
The light of surprise flashed in his eyes. Perhaps he had the impulse to investigate more thoroughly, but then, content with

gaining what he must have considered an unexpected victory, he said only, "Good."

Carite had announced the visit of the midwife, adding that there was nothing to fear or to worry about.

The master had left her precise instructions about what the woman could do. Under no circumstances, for example, would she be allowed to go as far as vaginal fumigation, checking the odor of my breath to confirm good communication between the uterus and the lungs, and hence my fertility.

The woman had a dark, wise look, and doubtless long experience in the type of examination requested by the future spouse or his family.

First she looked attentively at every detail of my face, every freckle and mole, and measured the width of the forehead and the skull. Then she inspected my body: hips, perhaps too narrow, they got a frown of disapproval out of her, while she seemed more satisfied by the muscle tone of my stomach and my arms and legs.

Meanwhile she asked me many questions: how old I was when I had my first menstruation, how often and of what type it was, did I have problems of digestion or changes of mood.

Then she told me to lie down on the bed.

Immediately I remembered the examination that Carite had had to perform, to ascertain my virginity, my fear as the hands of Master Domitian superimposed themselves on hers, searching between my legs, to reveal to me a sensation in which suffering was mixed with pleasure and shame, foretelling the end of childhood.

Now, instead, the fear had to do with a discovery not that I would make but, rather, the midwife and, with her, Valerian, Ennius Severus, and perhaps all Rome. While her fingers penetrated my body I was paralyzed by the thought that that exploration would reveal not a physical defect but, as if by magic, my lack of reserve, docility, and shame; unfitness for spinning and weaving; my wavering and at times superstitious religious sense. In other words, my unworthiness to marry Valerian. I was so persuaded of it that I began to tremble all over. The midwife stopped and asked if she was hurting me.

I gave her an imploring look. Perhaps the woman understood, and so she was merciful: covering my legs with my tunic, instead of keeping the verdict to herself she hastened to inform me that both the uterus and the cervix were normal.

Rosy-fingered dawn opened to the chariot of the sun not the gates of heaven but those of my heart, and I perceived what was happening around me through a light that made it both soft and incandescent.

I contemplated the world, forgetting myself in this or that corner of the house, as I would have forgotten some worthless object.

Finding me sitting and doing nothing Carite asked, "What are you doing there with that blank look?" And Pallante: "When you embrace Valerian I advise you to tell yourself that tomorrow he will die." I didn't even deign to look at him.

Or, prey to a sudden fear, I grabbed the zither and played for hours and hours, intensifying my abandon in the music, until Telifrone came to take it away from me, saying he couldn't listen anymore.

Toward every living being I felt tenderness and compassion, powerful and at the same time sweet, as if tempered by that hazy light.

Every morning I saw my mother leave for the opening of the temple of Isis and the rebirth of the sacred fire. She returned only toward evening, her eyes moist, her expression absorbed.

Then, when she had changed the garment of the worshipper for the matron's robe, I saw her dedicate herself resolutely to the preparations for my engagement.

The alternation of her moods, now associated with that of her garments, had never seemed to me so dramatic, and I embraced her suddenly, to surround her, too, with my halo of sweet light.

"What's the matter, what's happening to you?" she asked, surprised.

Then I kissed her face ardently, incapable of giving voice to a happiness that transformed apprehension and fear into treasure, and even fierce resentment into forgiveness.

My father, on the other hand, after our dialogue on marriage, I had seen only once, when, one night, finding it impossible to sleep, I had gone into the garden and he was entering the house. He told me to go back to bed and immediately went off, pursuing his own thoughts.

Just then the threat of famine was becoming more critical. And although the news of the shipwreck had been refuted, the ships carrying grain from Africa remained a mirage. In addition, fire had destroyed two of the most important storehouses of the Annona and my father had been unable to transfer to Ennius Severus the quantities necessary for the distribution of grain to the poor.

At the portico of Minucius there had been unrest among the recipients, discontented with a reduced ration and convinced that our leader's long absence from Rome was having dire effects.

None of these anxieties seeped into my meetings with Valerian, who had come to see me twice.

The first time, we exchanged only a few words, on the cold weather, I believe, which was unusual for Rome, and on the mosaic decorating the floor of the tablinum, which depicted a seascape.

Eyes fixed on the floor, I pointed to the figure of a large fish, saying, "Do you know it? It's a dolphin." Furious with myself, I had bitten my tongue for having uttered such a banality. He had smiled, brushing my neck with the index finger of one hand, and taken his leave.

The second time he stayed longer.

Again we sat in the tablinum, with the dolphin darting at our feet amid deep-blue waves. Valerian said that, at the time when he was superintendent of the mint, he had seen a coin made with a dolphin practically identical to that one. Then he told me how coins were made. I had never cared about such matters, and I was surprised to find them interesting. Perhaps it was the concise way in which he described the metals and the processes of casting, perhaps his casual, light tone. I thought, Well, he's not boring. Those who emphasize their own importance in what they say are boring. A little like me. I was about to tell him that, but held back. In the end, though, I told him, I said that in his words there was no trace of the rather moralistic vanity that I was often guilty of. He burst out laughing, then, suddenly serious again, asked me, "Are you sure?"

I nodded without adding anything, afraid of having already said too much. There was a long silence: I almost wished that he would go away, so that, alone, I could feel closer to him. And when he left I wanted to preserve my treasure, the image of his face, like the reflection of a divine presence.

On the wings of Love my brother had seen heaven and earth and had chosen not to be born. On the wings of Love I saw heaven and earth just emerging from the primal Chaos, separated out and molded by the hand of God, animated by his breath. I saw eternal springtime, while my soul lived in Valerian's, my beauty in his. With him I would be passionate about metals, mints, and coins; millstones, grindstones, and oil presses. For him I would descend to Hades; thanks to him, I, unique among women, would reascend to the light of day to join him in that celestial wheel visible to us alone. If something had threatened the perfection of it, the marvelous self-sufficiency, I would call on music, which could defend it like a fortress, amplifying every sigh and every heartbeat.

Then, from that height, I would contemplate with benevolence the struggle of mortal men and women.

On the eve of the betrothal, Ennius Severus died of an apoplectic stroke.

The wing of death was already spread over my happiness, but if Carite read in it a doomful sign and hurried to get a prediction of the future from the magician Theodorus, I found in Valerian's grief only a reason to love him more.

We therefore took off the robes of celebration and put on those of mourning to attend the funeral rites.

As night descended on the Forum and torches lighted the vast gathering of friends and relatives, certain dignitaries, among them my father, uttered eulogies for Ennius Severus on his funeral bed. I listened distractedly to their words, intent on observing Valerian, flanked by his brother, his two sisters, and the husband of one of them. I was struck by his impassive demeanor, the immobile face that betrayed not the least emotion. I admired him, comparing his firmness to the tears I would have shed if it had been my father. I remembered the rage that had possessed me after Lucilla's last miscarriage, my rebellion at the triumph of death, yet again holding us in check. I said to myself, "Look, even now Valerian has the wisdom to learn to die." Throughout the eulogies my future husband stared straight ahead, and, later, during the cremation ceremony, when his face was illumined by the leaping flames, I noted with a pinprick of sadness that not even for a moment did his eyes seek mine.

When the ships from Africa arrived, my father could finally deliver grain to the new Prefect of Grain Distribution. While that appeared to calm his anxieties and those of the city, it left my mother indifferent.

Because of the mourning, Valerian had cancelled the betrothal ceremony, letting us know, however, that his father's will had given precise instructions: if he died at the time of the marriage of one of his sons, after two weeks had passed the marriage was to be celebrated.

Two weeks was a short time, but, for the first time ignoring her proper duties, Lucilla completely forgot about the preparations for the ceremony. She went to the temple of Isis morning and night. She no longer touched wine or meat, or other foods considered impure, and refused to accompany my father to festivals or banquets. Mirrina said to Carite that she closed the door of her room every night, a useless precaution since, from the start of the last pregnancy, the master had given up his already rare visits.

I hadn't seen Valerian since the day of the funeral and I was tormented by doubts and fears. After all, the betrothal had not taken place and the matrimonial agreements had not been ratified. Perhaps with his father's death he had changed his mind about marrying me. Perhaps he had resolved to live with a concubine. Or perhaps, during the funeral ceremony, I had behaved in a way that displeased him. I re-examined my every gesture without finding anything important to reproach myself for. So I went to share my anxieties with my mother. At first she reassured me: if Valerian did not visit or write to me it was only because he must be very busy with matters having to do with the inheritance. There was no reason to think that he would cancel the pledges made by his father, I could be sure that, for him, too, the marriage was suitable from every point of view.

Then, perhaps judging that she had said what was necessary, she told me that every night Isis appeared to her in a dream. The goddess had heard the prayers she had tirelessly addressed to her after the days of the festival and, in her immense goodness, now meant to grant her children the grace of resurrection, and offer to Lucilla as well the certainty of life after death. She had then expressed the wish to initiate her into her mysteries: placing one foot on the threshold of Proserpina, Lucilla would reach the confines of death and return, passing through all the elements, and worshiping from close up the gods of the underworld and those of Heaven. More my mother could not reveal to me . . . And then, she sighed, the road was still long . . . A priest at the temple had agreed to help her with the rites of purification, accepting the confession of her sins, and prescribing ablutions and days of fasting and abstinence.

As she spoke I seemed to hear her grow increasingly distant, far away from me.

Only when she had uttered the last words did I understand that something extraordinary had happened, which for me was irremediable. The goddess with her cow horns had transmuted my greatest fear into a reason for Lucilla to live: illuminated by a supernatural grace, her dedication to her dead children would now overshadow all my desires and my sufferings.

Finally a letter from Valerian informed me that he would come to see me that afternoon.

He apologized for my not having heard from him, but he had been occupied by pressing obligations. The formal tone of the letter disappointed me. I read and reread it without finding the least trace of eagerness or expectation, not a single sweet or passionate word.

So I expected to see him weary and still distressed by the death of Ennius, but instead, dressed in his usual simple and elegant manner, his short beard carefully trimmed, he appeared relaxed. He asked about the preparations for the wedding with the same coldness that he might have shown toward the marriage of an acquaintance, showing a keen interest only in the fact that the traditional rites should be respected. He asked what my mother had arranged for.

"Everything," I said quickly, out of fear that he would subject me to more specific questions.

"Good," he said.

Then, without a kiss, without a caress, he left.

As soon as I was alone I wrote to Lucretia to give vent to my uneasiness: he no longer loved me, or he had never loved me. I found him strange, different from the young man I had seen for the first time with his father, and even more from the one who had later visited me. I needed to talk to her, could I see her as soon as possible?

My friend answered right away. And so, the next morning,

after a sleepless night, I went to see her, accompanied by Daphne.

After listening patiently to all my doubts, Lucretia said, "Look, Cecilia, I consider that the best you can expect from a husband is a minimum of affection and devotion, a minimum of respect. You know that I've never liked Carvilius, but I have no reason to complain of him. He's old, rather pedantic, he's a little too fond of the company of boys, but he's generous and patient, even if I still haven't given him a son. As you know, I'm not very enthusiastic about the idea of becoming a mother, and I admit that I do what's necessary to reduce as much as possible the risk of getting pregnant, even though he obviously doesn't know it. But one night when he seemed especially satisfied by the pleasure I'd given him, he confessed that, even without children, he would never want to divorce me. I have to say that I was moved, and I even felt a little guilty, because the truth is, after Aurelius, I had another lover. There's no guarantee that what you feel for Valerian will be reciprocated, because for you to love with your whole self, and more, won't be enough to be loved in return. So my advice is to rein in your passion. If your suspicions are well founded, and Valerian doesn't love you, at least you'll have better results if you hide your feelings."

How Lucretia had changed. With what skill she navigated between the cliffs of marriage and adultery! Yet she didn't show any disappointment, but in fact gave the impression of knowing how to get the best from every situation.

"In her way, she's wise," I thought, on the way home. "Whereas I'm nothing but a foolish girl."

A conversation I had a few hours later with Domitilla confirmed this verdict. She, too, appeared to me transformed, and not only because she was noticeably thinner. She told me that she was getting married at the end of the month, and that her future husband was much better than she would have expected.

His name was Sextus Cinna, and, being over forty, he had a second-rank post in the imperial chancellery. He was a man with little ambition: he was content with the career he had and would be content to marry her.

But my friend didn't speak with her usual bitterness; rather, she had a tone of sincere gratitude. She who had always known she didn't have those graces which, sought by men and exalted by poets, bring joy to girls' lives, she who had always been incapable of enjoying any pretense would find a refuge in marriage. She could be herself: honest and faithful. She would take care of the house and bring up the children, and if destiny did not reserve for her the knowledge of love, her family would at least honor and respect her.

In other words, everyone around me was changing, all learning to know themselves, perhaps becoming better, without the need for ridiculous stratagems like filling rolls and rolls of papyrus with confused thoughts and useless complaints. Abandoning them was the only sensible action I had taken for a long time. Besides, I disliked everything about myself, I was ashamed of not knowing how to appreciate what the present offered, of being always ready to torment myself with endless questioning.

I remembered something that Pallante had often repeated to me: "It's not events themselves that stir men up but the judgments men form about events." So I decided that until the day of my marriage I would utterly avoid indulging in any description, conjecture, or opinion that might trouble me. In practice, I would stop thinking. And so I did, first taking the precaution of telling my father that nothing had been arranged yet for the wedding.

In the course of two more visits from Valerian I said even less than I had earlier. Avoiding his gaze, which would have disturbed me, of his words I caught only what was indispensable in order to respond yes or no. When he left, and the fear of having behaved foolishly assailed me, I told myself that that fear, too, originated in a judgment, probably, like all my judgments, mistaken. Having taken a pledge not to think, distrusting the emotion that music or poetry would have inspired, I no longer knew how to pass the time. So I learned by heart the lists of barbarisms, or wore myself out with gymnastic exercises.

Since Valerian left for his lands in Campania I've been dreaming every night, and yet the gods seem to want to hide their prophecies in the recesses of real events.

Yesterday it was my wedding. No matter how extraordinary, the images of the dream are so vivid that they are superimposed on and confused with the memories of that day—images that increase anxiety and uncertainty, intensify the fragile state caused by my feelings for him.

Anyway, before dawn the room I'm in is suddenly illuminated by the dim opalescent light of Isis, and the goddess immediately approaches me, saying, "I am the mother."

While I look at her, filled with amazement, she leads me by the hand to a large mirror, where Lucilla, Carite, and Daphne are waiting for me.

With a bent spearhead, Isis divides my hair into six braids, then gathers them into a pointed bun. From Carite's hands she takes a flame-colored veil and covers my head and shoulders, from Daphne's a crown of myrtle and verbena, which she places on my head.

Then she calls my mother, ordering her to tighten the Hercules knot around my waist. She obeys, but instead of doubling the woolen belt she goes on winding it into a tangle.

Carite says, "The husband will never manage to untie it."

Isis says, "Lucilla is the mother. Lucilla knows."

Then the goddess disappears, leaving the room in darkness, and we are in the atrium, which is lighted by the rising sun, just at the moment when the augur raises the knife to sink it in the victim's neck. I avert my gaze, but Valerian holds my head in his hands, forcing me to look.

The augur goes on examining the sheep's entrails for an infinite amount of time. All are silent, but I hear their thoughts. I distinctly hear Carite and Telifrone praying that the signs be favorable. I hear the doubts crowding Domitilla's mind and my husband's increasing impatience. My father, however, is enveloped in a silence that I can't penetrate.

Suddenly there is a commotion. Without waiting for the augur's response, twenty unknown witnesses throng the altar to place the seal on the dowry agreements. I turn toward Lucretia, asking her anxiously how the omens are.

"Favorable," she says.

"Very favorable," says Valerian, taking me in his arms.

Then he whispers in my ear, "My sweet love, my wife."

I want to say, "So you love me . . ." but my lips move without articulating any sound, while my body trembles with happiness and gratitude.

Then Drusus appears: "In the end, just like Atalanta, you pick up the apple of Aphrodite. But now hurry, the wedding procession has almost arrived at your husband's house."

"Come on, climb up here, you'll be swifter than the wind!" Claudia meanwhile orders me, pushing me toward a catapult constructed out of a distaff and spindle, beside which my mother is waiting. She holds me as I climb up on the strange device, which launches us in flight over the crowded streets. A moment later, my mother opens her arms, dropping me into the center of the procession. "Where did you go?" Lucretia asks. "Juventus, Valerian's lover, is about to give him up forever."

Then, surrounded by a group of youths, a boy appears, carrying a heap of walnuts in his lifted tunic. He looks at me sadly, then, with an air of challenge, hugs his treasure tightly.

Arriving from the world of the dead to celebrate the wedding, the poet orders him:

Give her the walnuts,
unemployed page,
you've been playing for a long time now,
and it's good to serve
Talassius: give her the nuts.

Then, turning to my bridegroom, he continues:

Generous husband
they say that you're reluctant
to leave the young pages:
but you must, because it's best.
Hurrah, O Hymen,
god of weddings, hurrah.

Obeying a nod from Valerian, the boy gives the walnuts to the children, who immediately roll them so that they echo on the pavement. As the poet stops to observe them, I see spring dancing for the last time in his eyes full of longing. Then I see his quivering soul rise up and fly away, while I am carried by an infinity of arms across the threshold of my new house. I turn to look back, in search of my father. But he is far away, and his head is bent, so I can't see his tears. Instead I see the tears on the faces of Valerian and Juventus, as they exchange a last kiss. Suddenly I wake up.

"Come," Valerian said to me when we were in the room. I didn't move, enveloped in that air that was ours alone.

"Come," he repeated, and took my hand, touching my lips with a kiss. He loosened the crown of myrtle and verbena and, with a single gesture, the knot around my waist, which wasn't intricate like the one in the dream. Slowly he took off the veil, the tunic, then unbound all the swaddling and stepped back, letting his gaze linger on my shoulders, my breasts, my stomach, and along my legs. I shivered, brushed by a thousand subtle fingers.

"You're beautiful, Cecilia," he said, approaching. Gently he turned me, and kissed the hollow of my neck, just under the nape.

"This place is mine," he whispered, "don't ever forget it."

Again he took me by the hand, leading me toward the bed. He made me lie down, then he lay down beside me.

Every gesture seemed to extend in a soft, slow time that absorbed me, releasing me, body and soul, into a stupor. I was losing myself: was this what I had so feared?

If a caress kindled a flame at the center of my body, he withdrew until it was spent, exploring other places, other unknown hollows, lighting other fires, to again withdraw immediately.

He hadn't undressed, and my body crushed against his, immovable as a cliff. From a distance that could not be bridged, Valerian exposed my secrets, or, rather, induced me to reveal them, with knowledge and control.

Suddenly I opened my eyes, catching his eyes as they rested on my face. It was only a moment, but I was certain that through me he was contemplating his work. To erase it, I sought his lips, and then something startling happened: Valerian huddled in a corner of the bed, while a laugh, low and rhythmic like a kind of sob, began to shake his limbs. In his eyes was an astonishing light, such as might shine in the eyes of a demon, whether benign or evil I couldn't say, but not in those of a human being.

"What's wrong?" I asked, afraid.

He didn't answer, while the laugh continued to shake his body.

"You're frightening me," I said with a wail.

Then he came close and, kissing my face with burning tenderness, said, "Oh no, my love, don't be afraid. It's just my genie . . . He protects me, yes, but he's also evil, and sometimes it amuses him to make me do strange things. I'll tell him to stop, and I swear he'll never frighten you again."

How many unknown faces did I see filing by the following night, at the banquet? How many names did Valerian repeat to me, which I immediately forgot?

Of my first day in the house on the Palatine I've kept images bathed in color: the white of the *stola* that enveloped me, the ochre of the frescoes in the exedra, the silver of the olive trees in the garden. And the gilded partridges on the trays and the pink of the mullets.

"How is my little lady?" my father asked me suddenly. He was right beside me, and yet his voice, muffled by the noise of conversation, reached me from a distance. Maybe I answered, or maybe I simply nodded. I don't remember having uttered a single word during the entire dinner. I looked at the guests, each time isolating a detail of the face and its complexion. Who knows why Domitia, my husband's sister, took off her sapphire earrings, of a blue identical to her eyes, and laid them on a pillow, reminding me of the terrible Lamia, who every night puts her eyes in a bowl. One man, whom I often noticed later among those lined up each morning to greet Valerian, wore a ring on every finger, so that his hands sparkled, constantly creating new constellations.

Then I saw myself touring the house, guided by Benedetta, Valerian's nurse; he, it seemed, had left before dawn. I saw her lips move as she described to me one room after another, and although I tried to take in her words, I heard only the silence of the Palatine.

Suddenly someone raised a cup, and the toasts began. They called me chaste and cultured, and Valerian noble, honorable, and gracious. They hoped that the gods would give us more than three children, all healthy, so as to survive us.

The senator Lucius Portius Acilius, Prefect of the Games, recited verses he had composed on the occasion of the marriage of his protégé Valerian. A lawyer, whose name I don't remember, read a long plea in the case of suicide of a slave that he was particularly proud of.

I saw myself alone in the cold tablinum after Benedetta left. A strange inertia inhabited my body, transforming it into a cumbersome piece of furniture I didn't know where to put down. Reading, playing the zither, visiting a friend—my usual occupations seemed to me unnatural in all that silence. So I went out into the garden in the hope that at least there the noise of the city would reach me. Only a bird was singing in the depths of a cypress.

Another senator read a speech in which he strongly advised against allowing a free minor to pass to the guardianship of a freedman—a speech that years earlier the emperor in person had shown his appreciation of.

I noticed how all the speakers, although they were older than my husband, gave him deferential glances, as if needing his praise. Every so often I, too, turned to look at him, listening attentively, and, pale with shame, burning with desire, again saw his hands lightly touching my body. I quickly bent my head, convinced that on my face, in the blush of red and white, anyone could see what I felt. That marriage could have brought me such turmoil, an inextricable pleasure and pain, pleasure and pain that continuously changed one into the other, while a mysterious happiness enslaved me . . . In order not to think anymore, I forced myself to follow that boring, inescapable chatter. But how could Valerian devote so much attention to them?

Then his brother Tiburtius began the hortatory address of Agamemnon, who asks whether he must sacrifice his daughter

Iphigenia in order to gain the gods' favor for his fleet, but the master of rhetoric, Bebius Servianus, interrupted him. In honor of the bride, he proposed a higher challenge: the two brothers, who had been his best students, should engage in a real argument, calling on the guests to be the judges.

"Let's suppose the existence of a law prescribing that a priestess must be chaste and pure," the master proclaimed.

"We must have done this a thousand times," Valerian whispered in my ear.

But Bebio was already continuing, "A virgin, captured by pirates, is sold to a pimp who forces her to become a prostitute. The young woman asks the clients to pay her but respect her purity. A soldier refuses to grant her this mercy and uses violence against her, but she kills him. The girl, who is first charged, then acquitted and restored to her family, now asks to become a priestess. Valerian will argue in her favor, and Tiburtius against."

Hiding his irritation, my husband rose and, reaching the free side of the table, where the guests would see him clearly, began to declaim.

I am incapable of repeating all the arguments, the historical and legal subtleties, the mythological and literary examples that he brought to his speech. Most striking to me was the tone of his voice, skillfully modulated, as in a song, his knowledge of the pauses that would heighten expectation; the gestures of his hands, at once measured and persuasive; his facial expressions, never excessive or histrionic; and the way he moved away from the audience as if unconsciously, to suddenly turn and approach, evoking the thrust of a winning attack. Not a trace remained of the annoyance he had manifested at his teacher's proposal. Perfectly at his ease, strong and confident, Valerian pleaded in favor of that nonexistent outraged virgin as if he were speaking of a girl of flesh and blood, giving life to a fictitious world and inhabiting it with a naturalness that filled me with admiration and at the same time bewilderment.

Tiburtius, five years younger and surely less skilled, was not very convincing. He stumbled on words or pronounced them in an inappropriate tone, which emphasized the weakness of his arguments or revealed the artificiality of the entire debate, which he, unlike his brother, seemed deeply convinced of. And as if to fill the void of motivation, his miming was exaggerated: he twisted his lips, and kept looking up and down. Gradually, as one of the guests yawned and another began talking with his neighbor, I began to feel sorry for Tiburtius in his struggle to regain the guests' attention. I saw the exercise in all its point-lessness—an alarming thought, because it distanced me from Valerian, but then, remembering the annoyance with which he had received Bebius Servianus's suggestion, I felt reassured. If he lent himself graciously to that challenge it was only to please his old teacher.

The judges decided unanimously in favor of my husband.

With an obsequiousness that again struck me, Bebius raised his cup to Valerian, inviting the company to toast the perfect orator, to he who possesses every moral virtue.

I looked at Tiburtius, who at that eulogy hung his head.

Later, when Valerian was again lying beside me and, my anxiety dissipated by love, I told him of my admiration, he replied, "It's only a skill, you know . . . And at the same time it's all that the present offers us. You must have been aware of the absurdity of the argument, and yet I guarantee you there are some that are more inane. Anyway, it's no longer a matter of defending freedom or justice, but of celebrating and extolling the happiness that Rome has brought to peoples all over the world." He smiled mockingly.

"Why, don't you believe it's true?" I asked.

"Of course," he replied, serious again. "As Aelius Aristides said, ours is the best possible order, because we are rulers by nature. All those who exercised dominion before us were, by turns, masters and slaves of one another. We alone, free from the beginning, were born to govern. We have set up all the tools needed to achieve this goal, creating a political structure that no one possessed and imposing strict systems and rules; in satisfaction with and respect for these the freedom of the most diverse peoples is expressed. The emperor through his emissaries presides and watches over the unity and justice of the whole. And the result is not a cacophony of dissonant voices but a chorus that sings in unison, as if it were a single territory and a single people. Now the entire world appears to be rejoicing. He laid down his arms to devote himself in complete freedom to the beauty and joy of life. The cities have given up their ancient quarrels, and the spirit of competition animates them all: to appear the most beautiful and most prosperous. Thanks to the pax Romana, everywhere schools, fountains, and temples are built, everywhere our great culture sends up shoots and produces its fruits."

Again, as during the debate, he spoke with such intensity and persuasiveness that I believed that the earlier mocking smile had been the work of his spiteful genius. Yet, listening to him, I could not help thinking of our legions still engaged with the Quadi and the Marcomanni, who had no intention of exchanging their barbaric customs for the pax Romana, and I heard again Telifrone speak of his certainty that he lived in a world that was already dead. I was on the point of telling him this story, and asking him why Tiburtius had been so upset by his defeat, but I felt that I would risk marring that moment of harmony and tarnishing my image of Valerian, which, more than anything, I wished to keep bright and shining.

I soon realized that although Valerian was much younger than my father and held a less important office, he received three times the number of morning visits. Often the line wound outside the door of the house, and sometimes the door-keeper, with one excuse or another, denied entrance to certain petitioners. Some went away disappointed, others, irritated, remained waiting vainly in the cold or rain.

Having received his clients, my husband hurried to perform, in turn, his own duties, visiting this or that important personage, including, first of all, the Prefect of the Games, Portius Acilius, his patron and protector, who had been a great friend of Ennius Severus.

It happened that, in the whole day, I managed to see him only when he was leaving the house, sometimes by the back door in order to avoid the troublesome petitioners. He returned late, after the baths, barely in time to change for a dinner or reading we had been invited to.

On returning, if he had drunk a little too much he wouldn't come to my room, choosing to spend the night with me only after many days of absence. If I told him of my disappointment he reproached me for being nagging and disrespectful; if I concealed it behind diffidence or reserve he reproached me for being cold and distant.

Maybe he already had a lover. Or maybe he had never given up Juventus, or whatever his boy was called?

Upset, discouraged, I confided in Carite, who urged me not

to worry: until I had given him a son there was no danger that he would forget me.

Daphne, instead, suggested three potent aphrodisiacs that she herself had tried, following the advice of a sorceress, and which had had extraordinary results: five drops of an infusion of savory in a cup of water, a pinch of pepper mixed with seeds of stinging nettle sprinkled on roast meat, or ground St. John's wort dissolved in wine. If those weren't enough to rouse the master's ardor she would take me to a Hyperboreus, who knew an infallible remedy. One night Daphne had seen him fulfill the desire of a girl in love with a certain Pancrate who wanted nothing to do with her. With her own eyes she had seen him call Hecate up from Hades, with Cerberus on a leash, and pull the moon down from the sky, and change into a woman, then into a beautiful heifer, and finally into a small dog. She had seen him mold mud into a little cupid and order him, "Go, and bring Pancrate here." And with her own eyes, right afterward, she had seen Pancrate running to the girl and throwing his arms around her neck. The two were locked in a room and remained together until the rooster crowed. Then the moon flew up to the sky and Hecate sank beneath the earth.

But I was still the daughter of a doctor and philosopher, and at the mere idea of resorting to spells or witches' potions I felt ashamed. Above all, though I knew it was a fable, I recalled the metamorphosis of poor Lucius, and feared that the gods would punish my audacity and shamelessness by changing Valerian into an ass. So I decided to go see Lucretia, who, her feet now planted firmly on the ground, would give me the best advice.

As soon as I confessed my anxieties she burst out laughing: "What can I tell you: in Rome love is out of fashion, and all men are cultivating abstinence, some too involved in their career or in philosophy, some wanting to be sure to send into the world a strong, healthy heir. From what you tell me, for instance, Valerian seems to behave just like Carvilius. Since I haven't gotten pregnant yet, my husband went to a doctor, who prescribed a series of hygienic rules. In the first place, he is to avoid excessive work, mood changes, and anger and joy. To control his breathing and make it more powerful, he declaims epics every morning, and I assure you that it is comical to hear his voice going suddenly from low-pitched tones to ear-piercing high ones. But the most important aspect, and for me the most pleasant, is that he is not to have relations too frequently, because they tire the body and the mind and disperse the seed that, in order to be fertile, has to be thick and abundant. It was Carvilius himself who explained all this to me. With a disarming ingenuousness he also confessed that before intercourse he always takes a walk or a horseback ride, and, to make sure the sperm have the necessary quantity of air, eats flatulent foods, such as fava beans, octopus, pine nuts, chickpeas, flaxseed, and rughetta. The trouble is that while he used to be rather lazy and absent-minded, now he is so vigilant and determined that I had to give up diaphragms and poultices, for fear that he would notice. You'll see, thanks to that zealous doctor I'll end up pregnant, and if I don't die in childbirth I'll get fat and ugly like any married woman."

I told her that I would like to have a child, partly because it would keep me company. It was strange: I loved my husband, and yet I had never felt so alone. I missed my parents, especially my father, and even with Telifrone and Carite things had changed so much that they no longer seemed themselves. Or perhaps it was Telifrone and Carite who no longer saw me as Cecilia. My pedagogue no longer waited for me every morning to make me do my exercises. I had to go find him in his room, where he retreated to study hermetic texts or pray.

And Carite was less affectionate: I seldom found her at home and, when she was there, she often had a serious, absorbed expression that was unfamiliar to me.

So, after reluctantly occupying myself with the shopping for the house, unable to find a use for all the money my husband gave me, I passed the time waiting for his return in a restless indolence: if I read to myself my voice soon grew feeble and died, and the same happened with the zither. Constantly restless, like a spinning top, I went through the house again and again, without finding anything that captured my attention.

What was the use of my education in grammar and philosophy if I now found myself at a dead end, my head full of fine words and my soul in turmoil: a pot in which every sort of affection and inclination boiled, but not a pinch of those gifts which would have made me a good wife?

Then, I don't know why, I asked my friend if she ever thought of Aurelius.

Lucretia smiled, she said that yes, of course, he often returned to her mind, but as if in a fog. Only a few months had passed and yet, seeing what she had been then, she had a hard time recognizing herself. It wasn't Aurelius she missed but the bold and passionate girl he had revealed to her, and who, at least for a moment, had been lost in important foolishness. "Just what's happening to you now," she concluded. "You've changed, Cecilia, Love has enslaved you."

Who knows if one day I, too, would think of the wound the god had inflicted, of the trembling wait for Valerian, as important foolishness. At that moment I wished to be already grayhaired and tottering, to look back at the faded traces of my youth.

My husband's horses, competing for the faction of the Greens, were to be driven by Attalus, the charioteer who at only twenty had won more than a hundred victories and whose portrait adorned walls along all the streets.

So, early in the morning, I went with Daphne to the Circus Maximus, where Valerian would be arriving with the procession that left from the temple of Jove on the Capitoline.

I went once, two years ago, with my father to an arena, and had always refused to go back. However relieved I was to learn that it would not be gladiatorial combat or wild beasts fighting, as soon as I entered the Circus I was intimidated by the immense crowd in the stands, roaring as it waited for the sacred procession. Quivering, it seemed a Hydra with a thousand heads, twisting its heavy tentacles and making the wooden stands creak. From the tribune of honor I could sometimes isolate a detail of that vibrant mass—the blue standards of the Veneta faction and, farther away, the white ones of the Albata, a noisy knot of bettors, the smoke rising from the stands selling roast meat under the arcades—and for a moment the thought of men and women of flesh and blood was enough to calm me.

But when Porcius Acilius entered in the winners' chariot, surrounded by priests and statues of the gods and emperors, every detail disappeared and, with it, every human being, reabsorbed into that single body from which a roar of jubilation and acclaim now rose and thousands of banners waved.

Among the magistrates and clients behind the prefect, I thought I recognized Valerian, his back straight, his head slightly inclined in a serious pose, and, beside him, his brother Tiburtius. Not even during the sacrifice did the clamor of the crowd, indifferent to the ritual and concentrated in fretful expectation, diminish. Then Portius's purple toga and ivory scepter moved, and the procession of dignitaries reached the tribune of honor. Valerian and Tiburtius took their places beside me, while the chariots waited at the starting line and the horses pawed the ground.

The charioteers were struggling to keep them reined in, when the sound of the trumpets was heard and the prefect let the white flag fall into the arena. A cloud of dust rose, the hooves beat the sand with a sound of barbarian drums, and the public, delirious by now, shouted out the names of the champions, men and beasts.

My husband's horses, Victor and Polydoxus, started off with a momentum that immediately seemed excessive, violently freeing themselves from the two middle horses tied to the yoke, and dangerously close to breaking the harness and hurling the driver out of the chariot. I turned to look at Valerian: his face was contracted, his fists clenched at his sides in the effort to master himself. His brother, on the other hand, was impassive. Although the young Attalus managed to regain control and pass his rivals halfway around the first lap, even I could see that the animals, their necks foaming with sweat, seemed to be responding not to him but to some demon that had possessed them. Suddenly lethargic, they slowed their pace, and then, without warning, hurtled forward, bellies to the ground, threatening to rip the harness.

"What's the matter with them?" Valerian exclaimed, no longer taking care to hide his apprehension. Meanwhile, the supporters of the Greens shouted encouragement to their beloved champion. It was terrible to see that body, which had an extraordinary strength and agility, tossed from one side of the chariot to the other like a rag doll. At one point he was about to fall, but, gripping the reins and making a prodigious leap, he managed to stay on his feet, while the crowd exploded in a cry of fear and relief. Coolly he guided the chariot to the outside, risking losing ground and at the same time giving the horses' fury an outlet. On the fourth lap, Victor and Polydoxus, swift as the wind, had infected the other two, and the Greens had returned to the lead amid the cheers of Valerian and his people. I was still holding my breath as I followed the race when Polydoxus stopped dead, just at the center of the curve, bringing the chariot to a standstill. The horses of the Red faction, who were close behind, couldn't swerve, and violently crashed into it.

Attalus was thrown in the air and fell to the ground, the reins that he hadn't had time to cut still wrapped around his chest. While Polydoxus, whose bridle had snapped, ran wildly, causing confusion among the chariots, the driver was dragged around the track by the maddened beasts. Before the men of the Greens could stop them they had taken three laps, and the body of the champion was a mass of sand and blood. Valerian's eyes filled with tears and I took his hand. He turned to me, whispering between his teeth something I couldn't understand.

When it was clear that Attalus was dead, the men lifted him onto their shoulders with the honors due a valiant soldier, carrying him first in front of the tribune for the final farewell to the magistrates, then out of the Circus. The crowd was silent. For a moment I seemed to perceive the gaze of those thousands of eyes as they followed the remains of that suddenly extinguished star. And I remembered what Drusus had said to me one day about the Circus: if I despised the races it was only because I was ignorant of their deep significance, the complex cosmology that they put on display before the eyes of the people. The channel of the Euripus surrounded the arena as the sea surrounds the earth, the obelisk was the sun at its zenith; the twelve doors of the stalls represented the constellations, the seven laps of the course the succession of the days of the week, and the race of the chariots the route of the sun. According to Drusus, the fear and rapture of the spectators, the jubilation and frenzy that frightened me, could be explained by the tragedy of the cosmos that was taking place before their eyes: the mystery of the eternal birth and death of all things was no longer unfolding in a remote Hyperuranium but literally at their feet, and as if in miniature, rendering comprehensible what usually stood above them. At the passing of every chariot, the spectators rejoiced at the birth of a new day, while if a charioteer perished they could weep for a sun that had been extinguished, as they wept now for the young champion.

Waiting for me at home was a letter from my father, summoning me that very afternoon. I was disturbed by the death of Attalus, and the urgent tone of the letter increased my anxiety, so, without having any food, I ordered the litter to take me to my parents' right away.

I found my father walking up and down in the tablinum. He stopped only to give me a quick kiss, then resumed his pacing as he related what had happened.

For several days Lucilla's health had been showing worrying signs. Keeping to a diet that was not very nourishing, she had become noticeably thinner. More and more often she lost her voice and suffered choking fits and convulsions, followed by an extended paralysis.

In spite of that, as soon as she recovered she insisted on going to the temple of Isis, where she now spent the night as well, waiting for the goddess to visit her in her dreams. During these apparitions Isis had often expressed the desire to initiate her into her mysteries, and yet she delayed giving precise instructions. This uncertainty tormented my mother, but when my father suggested that she rest and stop visiting the temple for a few days, she began sobbing, and then, again, her breathing failed and she fainted. In those episodes my father recognized an illness of women, which often struck those who couldn't get pregnant or carry a pregnancy to term. Most unfortunate, though, there was just one known remedy, and Lucilla could be treated only at the cost of new suffering, if not of her life. He spent the days preoccupied with feeding thousands of Romans, and neglected his own wife. Above all he was a doctor and, no matter how hard he tried, he couldn't master the sense of impotence brought on by the affliction of one so dear to him.

I had never heard him speak in such a sorrowful tone, and with such despair. The protector, the savior seemed to me a helpless man. I felt sorry for him, and yet an unknown, and odious, fear kept me from embracing him.

When I went to my mother's room what I saw from the doorway filled me with horror. She was sitting in front of the mirror, and Mirrina was cutting her marvelous hair. Half of her head was already shaved, while on the other there were a few disheveled tufts. Her face, thin and very pale, seemed a mask where comic and tragic features were mixed randomly on the same side. I approached, placing a hand on her shoulder. She barely turned her head, and a weak smile was outlined on her lips.

"What are you doing?" I asked foolishly.

Without interrupting the work of her maid, my mother explained to me that that night she had had a vision. She was in the temple, at the feet of the statue of the goddess, when she had heard someone gasping for breath. She had looked around, but the place seemed perfectly deserted. Then the gasping stopped, and a child a few years old appeared, calling her by name.

"Annia," my mother had answered, holding out her arms to welcome her, but the child continued to look at her without moving. Her features were not those of her daughter and yet, as happens in dreams, she was certain that it was her.

"Annia, my child," she had repeated.

The girl had shied away, and in a teasing voice had said, "You know, My Lady, my mother doesn't want to get better, and so I can't be reborn. If she doesn't get better I will continue to wander in the darkness, in this dark world of the dead, without ever finding my toys or catching my bird who's flying around, blind and demented. My Lady, do you know my mother? If you know her tell her that she must get well, our great mother wants her to, she who instructed me to come and tell you: 'One cannot serve with a sick mind and body the being who is absolutely pure and immaculate.' Will you remember that? I implore you: tell my mother to be quick, I can't breathe down here, and I am so afraid of the dark." Then Annia vanished.

My mother said that, in her bouts of asphyxia, it was her child who was slowly suffocating, day by day, because she was still living in sin. The goddess had finally given a clear answer. Confession and abstinence from certain foods and pleasures were no longer enough: salvation for her and her children could be reached only through expiation and tireless purification.

While Mirrina ended her work, and Lucilla's head shone white as a skull, I went away without saying a word.

On the way home I prayed for her, for my father, for my unhappy love. But instead of flying away, the words fell like rocks into a bottomless well, with no echo, so that no god would have heard them.

I hadn't yet fallen asleep last night when the noise of the carriage and horses, and the shuffling of servants carrying trunks, announced Valerian's return from Campania. I waited a while for him to come to me, until I heard his footsteps go by my room.

When I woke up, Benedetta told me that the master had gone out early, giving orders to the doorkeeper to put off all visits until tomorrow.

Later, as I was passing the closed curtain of the tablinum, I heard Valerian talking to a man whose voice was unknown to me. In an inflexible tone he was saying that the term of the loan had been agreed on from the beginning, and that for no reason did he intend to extend it. When the other continued to beg him, asking for a month more, he cut off the discussion, threatening to sell the debt to someone who would know how to get paid back here and now. Then he called the doorkeeper, I suppose to lead him out, and I hurried out into the garden.

I remembered I had once heard a broker thank my father for the patience and trust he had shown in granting him an extension. I compared my father's compassion, his kindness, with the harshness of my husband, who apart from everything else seemed to have no qualms about doing business with men who were less than honest.

So when Benedetta came to tell me that the master wanted to speak to me, after waiting so long I was afraid to see him.

Valerian greeted me with a kiss, asking how I had spent the days, if in his absence I had seen my parents and my friends, if I was satisfied with the servants and the house. Then he announced that he intended to give a dinner and wished to consult with me about the guests. He took a pen and tablet, stretched out on the couch and began, "So. Naturally Portius Acilius and his concubine. My old teacher Bebius Servianus — no, he's really too pedantic . . . Ah, both Quintilians are in Rome, and it would be a pleasure to receive them. And then Petronius, the Prefect of Grain Distribution, with his wife . . ."

"Your sisters and Tiburtius . . ." I said, thinking to anticipate him.

"No, Tiburtius no."

"Why?" I asked, surprised.

Valerian hesitated: it was obvious that talking about this annoyed him.

"In the country we argued again about the boundaries of our properties . . . He refuses to give me a small lot where I would be able to dig a well. After all I've done for him . . ." he broke off, biting his clenched fist. He seemed about to burst into tears, just like a child, and it moved me so much that I went to embrace him. But Valerian stopped me with a gesture: "Cecilia, I don't like you to be worried about me."

Discouraged and confused, I bowed my head, and he continued.

"Tiburtius is an ingrate, and unworthy to bear our name. All he does is go around with charlatans and boys, squandering his patrimony on dubious banquets. Then he rushes about trying to get favors from anyone he meets to obtain some kind of position; he starts a thousand things and finishes none, he's always anxious and discontent. In short, I've already done everything I can for him: now he has to manage on his own. So we won't invite Tiburtius. Naturally my sisters, yes, and your father and mother . . ."

I said nothing, but then, perceiving a new danger, I had the wit to tell him that Lucilla wasn't well.

"What's wrong? I'm sorry . . ." And he looked up at me.

"Nothing serious, I think . . . Only I don't know if she'll have recovered so soon."

"Then your father," he said, eliminating Lucilla from the list.

I doubted that he would accept, since she had gotten so much worse lately, but I preferred to say nothing, and yet hated myself for my silence. I challenged him: "I would like to invite Lucretia and her husband . . ."

Again Valerian looked at me: "I don't know what you find in her . . . You can read her every thought in her face."

"We've been friends since we were children."

"Yes, but surely you don't want to inflict on me that mediocre Carvilius, who can't do anything but quote Martial with every new course. No, listen, let's invite Claudia and Manlius. At least he'll tell us about the follies of Commodus among the Marcomanni."

I thought: you are the vulgar one, but I didn't say it. Instead I said, "Let's invite Domitilla and her husband."

"Yes, Sextus Cinna is a simple, modest man, I don't dislike him. And the doorkeeper told me that during my absence he came by to greet me."

I wondered what Sextus could want from Valerian. Maybe he was in trouble, or maybe Domitilla was wrong in considering him unambitious. My husband then ended the list with the usual names, a small court that included certain recent acquaintances—bright stars of his firmament, some of whom I had already seen set in the span of a short time—but above all childhood friends and school companions, who had in common meek, gentle manners, a rank inferior to his, and an adoration for him mixed with fear.

I realized that his old friend Pliny was missing from the list, and I asked why.

"No, Pliny won't come. I don't intend to see him anymore. A year ago I made him a loan, without interest, and he still pretends not to remember."

"You could tell him . . ."

"Such things are not said . . . And anyway I was already starting to like him less."

He put down the pen and the tablet, got up and came to me, holding me around the waist. "I missed you, Cecilia . . . I missed your voice. Will you play something for me? Yes, love, sing of the wandering moon and the labors of the Sun on your golden zither."

As I sing an Egyptian melody for Valerian, the features of my face slowly fade, my hair falls in locks to the grass, and finally my whole body dissolves into air, leaving only the voice, which begins to whistle among the branches like a furious wind.

"Cecilia, turn back," say the Nymphs, "you're already at the end of the story, and yet it's hardly begun. In revenge for your mockery, for entertaining Juno with long talks while Jove coupled with us, she has condemned you to speak in short phrases, repeating only the final part of a speech, echoing the words. But you are not yet deprived of your body. Hurry to retrieve it if you want to find Valerian!"

I woke up filled with anguish, crying "Valerian!" and now I'm sure that the dream contains a grim omen. Like Echo, I will dissolve into pure voice, perhaps because it's the only thing about me that my husband really loves. Further, I will be compelled to repeat only the words of others. But when will it happen? And through what divine intervention?

Or perhaps the vision reveals what is already happening: in the song, even in the papyruses, all I do is repeat sounds, verses, thoughts read or heard around me . . .

I am no longer anyone, I really am nothing. That strange lightness that the presence of Annia gave me has vanished. I've lost you, too, dear sister.

Sometimes he's tender and ardent, sometimes cold and occupied exclusively with himself. His affection then seems to retreat, like a fire doomed to fade and be extinguished in the enclosure of his heart. Generous, loving, he becomes irritated at some trifle and suddenly announces his contempt and the death of an old friendship. Or he harbors secret, inadmissible rancors, as if he were clouded by the shadow that he himself casts on his enemy, especially if someone is close to him, like his brother Tiburtius. In short, he is volatile and, as with Lucilla, I never know what to expect from him or how to behave. With every passing day I feel more alone. And then I am numbed by a sort of inertia that prevents me even from bringing some comfort to my parents.

Today I confided in Carite. I told her that my mother was worse, and about my father's suffering. Both immersed in their troubles, they seem to have forgotten me.

"Not even you, Carite, love me anymore," I said to her. "Since we've lived here you've been distant, almost evasive. Are you hiding something from me?"

"What should I hide from you? That the affection for a daughter never changes, my child? Every day I pray to God that he will soon let you know this love, with its invincible force, and protect your weakness."

Later, as I was leaving to go to my parents, I ran into Tiburtius, who, outside, was arguing with the doorkeeper. Our gazes met, while the man was insisting that Valerian had deliberately given orders not to let him in.

Uneasy, uncertain what to do, I stood on the threshold. Tiburtius took advantage to try to force his way in, but was immediately stopped by the doorkeeper, a tall, heavily built man, who easily dragged him out and pinned him against the wall. Panting and weak, the young man shouted at him to take his hands off, without heeding the passersby who looked at them with curiosity. At the sight of a young man in a purple-trimmed toga being shoved around by a servant, some barely restrained a mocking smile.

"Let me go or you'll get a hundred lashes," he cried, unable to free himself from the man's grasp.

"Who's going to give them?" the doorkeeper replied, insolently, while the eyes of the unfortunate young man filled with tears.

When I ordered the doorkeeper to let him go, he reluctantly obeyed. I approached my brother-in-law, who was nervously readjusting the cloak over his shoulders. In a low voice I said, "I'm sorry, Tiburtius."

He gave me a hard look, then answered, "It's I who am sorry for you. And you don't know how sorry, Cecilia."

Then he hurried off.

As the litter carried me to Trastevere, I couldn't stop

reviewing in my mind the scene I had just witnessed. Perhaps I should speak to Valerian, intercede for his brother, find the arguments that would soothe his resentment. Yes, I would do it that evening, but meanwhile I had to think of what awaited me at my parents' house, concentrate on what I would say to them.

If I was destined to become a voice, as the oracle had announced, why not interpret it in a favorable sense, forgetting at least for a day that I was condemned only to repeat? Yet the more I reflected, the more it appeared to me unjust. What had I done to deserve such a punishment? Certainly I was not a model wife, at times in my thoughts I was irreverent toward Valerian and had doubts about him, but Juno could not reproach me for not loving him. Or perhaps even now I was giving evidence of superstition, I was complaining about the gods, judging them capricious and cruel, instead of bearing up and freeing myself from that stuttering diffidence in which I had been flailing since my wedding day.

The unhappy look with which my father received me compelled me, more than all my thoughts, to find some courage.

"You don't know how I miss you, my little lady," he said, hugging me tight. "At night, the rare times when I manage to sleep, I wake up suddenly thinking of you. During the day, my legs carry me to your empty room as if they had a will of their own. Then, sadly, I return, as if I had been driven out."

I was about to tell him how much I missed him, too, but I restrained myself in order not to increase his distress. When he asked about my health and Valerian's, I said that we were fine and that everything was going very well. Then he took my chin between thumb and index finger and, forcing me to look at him, asked if I was hiding something.

Firm in my purpose, I said that Valerian was a very affectionate husband. For once, my words sounded convincing even to my ear, and he nodded with a more serene air.

He cleared his throat, then began:

"I've made an important decision, Cecilia, and I don't want to put off sharing it with you, although you mustn't yet talk to your mother about it. Marcus Aurelius let me know from Germany that he intends to renew my nomination as Prefect of the Annona. As you can imagine, I thought about it for a long time, evaluating every aspect of the matter. In the end I've decided to give up the honor that our prince has had the kindness to bestow. It's not for me to say if I have served Rome adequately, if I have done my part in the exchange of favors among men that social life requires, but ever since I started on a public career, and, even more, since I've become prefect, I've led an existence filled with responsibilities and worries, burdened by the weight of the high office that I represent. For that, and for the family patrimony, I abandoned the practice of medicine, I neglected my studies, while philosophy has been reduced to an occasional exchange with Pallante—who will not in his heart approve of my choice. Although I've kept in mind the proof of every precept, I have continued to break them all. I know how to explain why one must not lie, flatter, or betray, and yet every day I lie, flatter, betray. In the morning as soon as I see the line of clients waiting for me in the atrium I seem to hear the words of the great Horace: 'A rich patron dictates the law as a good mother would, and exacts more wisdom and virtue than he has himself.' There, I am that patron, very rich and, indeed, increasingly less wise and less virtuous. In addition, your mother's health compels me to devote constant care to her, providing treatments that the bad air of Rome seems to make useless. So I am convinced that a change of climate will help her. I've already done what is necessary to leave you this house, to free the slaves who live here and free myself of the management of all the properties until you inherit them. Afterward, it will be up to you, to you and your husband, to decide what to do. I've kept only the villa in Umbria, where Lucilla and I will go and live as soon as possible. Naturally, you will be welcomed with open arms whenever you want to visit us."

"Have you nothing to say, Cecilia?" he added after a bit, since I was silent.

I shook my head, then in a whisper said I agreed with his decision, sure that a change of life would be good for both of them, while the mere thought of remaining in Rome without them filled me with anguish.

Luckily my mother was sleeping, and I didn't have to face her, too, and conceal what awaited her.

But now I wonder: how will Lucilla take it? Leaving the temple will cure her or lose her forever. I'm also disturbed by what my father said, quoting Horace: "I am that patron, very rich and, indeed, increasingly less wise and less virtuous." It troubles me that all this time there can have been another Paulus, different from my father, a Paulus Prefect of the Annona who lied, flattered, and betrayed.

What worries me, finally, is Valerian's reaction. Yet again I will have to find the right words, but I know that, however precise and tranquil, they will not serve to prevent his censure.

The moon has set, disappearing from the window of my room to wrap itself in the mantle of Night, and yet I still can't sleep. How I long for the moments when it was the anxious wait for Valerian that kept me from sleeping! Now it's pain, like a vise on my stomach, holding mind and body awake. If I try to lie down on my bed the grip gets tighter until it takes away my breath. So I walk up and down, as many steps as separate me from the most remote province of the Empire, so as to wear out my limbs and make them silent.

Yesterday, when I got home, I found a letter from Claudia's sister saying that, after four days of labor, my friend had given birth, but the infant had died a few hours later. She herself was very ill, and had asked to see me.

On foot, alone, I immediately went to her.

When I entered her room Claudia turned her head toward me, holding out her hand weakly.

"If souls still live, after the body is gone, my baby lives, but without me . . ." she whispered.

I sat on the bed and caressed her forehead, without finding the power to speak.

"And so every moment I pray to my son to take me with him. The moment is coming, Cecilia, and soon we'll be together. But you who have always been so good with words, promise me you'll persuade Manlius and his family not to engrave on the tomb his name or how long he lived . . . Reading it, even from up there, the pain in my heart would be too much to bear."

Swallowing my tears, I assured her that I would do as she wished. I searched my memory for a thought, a phrase that might soothe her, but how could I tell her that all that suffering was indifferent, how deny the omnipresence of evil, its invincible force? It would be better to tell her about Isis, and her love for her brother-spouse, which in the end gained for him life after death.

Suddenly Claudia began to recite, in a monotone, "'Queen Juno, if fortune can be even more propitious for the citizens of Rome, let us entreat and implore you. Let us, the hundred and nine mothers of families of the citizens of Rome, all married, ask that you increase the power and sovereignty of the citizens of Rome, at home and abroad . . .' See how well I learned? And yet Juno . . ." She laughed quietly.

After a pause she added, "They let me hold him in my arms for a moment, you know, and he was alive . . . His little feet moved. I heard him breathe . . . Cecilia, do you really think I'll find him again?"

Overwhelmed by grief, or perhaps by the love that always makes hope bud in our hearts, for a moment I saw them together, mother and child, in the quiet gathering of souls, freed from the chains of the body and from death.

And leaning over to kiss her cheek I told her that I was sure.

A h, I can imagine the emperor's face as he reads your father's letter!" and the usual little mocking laugh escaped Valerian.

"A magistrate who leaves the service of Rome, who takes for himself the freedom that to Caesar is denied! To do what? Devote himself to philosophy . . . He will despise him, but in his heart he'll be envious. However, your father has made a great mistake: just now when the barbarians are increasing the pressure on the frontiers we need to be reinforcing Rome, expanding the Empire, not withdrawing into ourselves to care for our own little souls! Not to mention that ridiculous idea of freeing the slaves all at once. Of delegating to others the administration of properties. Already I seem to hear the talk of the whole city . . . In regard to me, Paulus has played a dirty trick: in the first place because his decision is doomed to darken the image of the whole family, and then because I was counting on him to obtain the appointment to questor three years early. Asking Portius Acilius for help is always possible, although there's a risk of becoming too dependent . . . But, anyway, Cecilia, I will love you just the same," he concluded, giving me a kiss.

Slightly reassured by these last words, I confided to him how much the death of Claudia grieved me, that I couldn't sleep thinking of her and her child and that I had written to Manlius Cornelius to ask him not to engrave the name of the infant on the tomb—as my friend wished—but he hadn't answered. "Imagine . . ." Valerian commented, then he held me in his arms, rocking me for a long time.

In that moment of unexpected tenderness I found the courage to speak to him about Tiburtius, but he immediately darkened.

"You know I don't intend to see him anymore . . . Now that my father is dead I don't have to play the comedy of brotherly love. Tiburtius has always hated me, because I was the favorite of both our parents. Since childhood he's never missed a chance to display his resentment, but, being timid and cowardly by nature, he has always used a low blow, a knife in the back. Now too many rumors are circulating about him, and in particular one that directly concerns me . . . You remember the race? How strange the horses were?"

I nodded. But he seemed to hesitate, then he abruptly concluded that it was better not to talk about it, that first he had to be sure about what had happened.

I see Claudia again, and her eyes that are begging not to live but to die, to be reunited with her child. I leaned over for a last kiss, to encourage in her a hope that, since the time when I used to write to Annia, has been extinguished in my heart, and whose loss I feel sometimes like a mutilation. A life after life? Reuniting with the souls of those we have loved? Affections that endure into eternity?

In Valerian's library I found the poem of Lucretius.

Even if time reunited our matter
after death, and ordered it again as it is now arranged,
and also the light of life were restored to us,
still not one of these facts would have to do with us,
once the thread of our consciousness is broken.
Now nothing of us matters to us, such as we were before,
no suffering grips us from those previous existences.

If with death God did not grant Claudia the mercy of finding her child, did he at least have the compassion to erase in her every memory?

Tonight, feeling sad, I started reading again at random, and came upon these lines:

When finally the lovers with limbs entwined enjoy the
[flower
of youth, and already the body foretastes pleasure,
and Venus is on the point of pouring the seed into
[the feminine field,
breasts eagerly press together, the saliva of mouths is mixed,
and they pant biting each other's lips;
in vain, because they can't detach anything of the
[beloved person,
or penetrate and lose themselves with all their limbs
[in the other body.

As the beauty of those words made their truth bitter, I felt a growing impulse to be free of them, and suddenly I threw the book on the bed and got up to go to Valerian. I wanted him to prove them wrong with his caresses, with kisses heal the wound of our distance.

It was so late that I went quickly toward his room, sure of finding him. Reaching the middle of the atrium I heard a soft laugh, and recognized Daphne coming out, closing the door quietly.

I cling to my nurse.

Suddenly I am a child again, feeling the tenderness with which she holds me to her breast. The good smell of her milk, the singsong sound, soft and hard, of the Greek of her first lullabies. I feel the same unbearable torment—immobilized from head to foot by thick, rough wool swaddling, saturated with my excrement—and she who hurries to free me, to unwind the swaddling and bathe me, massage my body, spreading an ointment on the sores.

She takes me in her arms and, with a magic formula chasing away the horrible Lamia, devourer of infants, sings to me softly. As she is doing now. And I, who preserve no memory of that time, suddenly find again the comfort that the hands, the breast, and the voice of my nurse gave me then. Wearied by weeping, exhausted, I let myself relax into that peace and finally fall asleep.

"Cecilia, aren't they all like him! In fact, the exception is your father, who years ago gave up touching the slaves and insisted on living without sin. I understand your disappointment, and even the jealousy a little, but if it weren't that you still didn't have a child, I assure you that it would be a liberation not to constantly have around you a husband in love. I shouldn't have to tell you this, because you know it yourself: the important thing now is for you to get pregnant, and before someone else does. Luckily the master made sure in the nuptial agreements that Valerian is forbidden to take a concubine, but still it would be more prudent not to waste time."

So my nurse advised me and yet, every time Valerian knocked at my door, I pretended to be asleep, thinking with bitterness of what Lucretia had said about semen, which, to be fertile, shouldn't be scattered.

With Daphne I behave as usual, as if unaware of anything. But I continually observe her handsome face, spying the traces of a fleeting love, kisses and caresses that do no harm, in the mad desire that lips wounded by passion be reserved for me. One minute I decide to dismiss my maid, ending my self-inflicted torture, the next I detain her, in order to feel closer to him.

My parents are about to leave Rome and then my solitude will be complete. Needing to confide my feelings to someone and not knowing where to turn, I went to look for Telifrone in his room. But through the closed door I heard him praying, and so I gave it up.

One room after another was emptied, as in a last breath that hovers in the air for a time, vibrating with the sounds of the past.

I followed my father through the house while he gave orders to the slaves, deciding without hesitation or regret what to leave behind. The calm that had always been a relief to me wounded me at this solemn moment, and I was quick to leave him, to join Lucilla, imagining she was as broken-hearted as me, if for different reasons.

Her shaved head covered by a veil, she had sunk down on the only seat remaining in the tablinum and was staring with an unquiet gaze at the void in front of her, as if wishing to divine what the future had in store for her. With a darting glance, like a hunted animal, she made sure that my presence did not threaten her, then, turning to look at the emptiness, she said, "I'm afraid to leave the temple, even though the priest assured me that distance will in no way prejudice my devotion. The goddess's orders are carried out everywhere, and although it's farther away, there is a temple of Isis in Montovolo, where it will be possible to stay when I feel it's necessary . . . But not being able to take part every morning in the opening of the temple, the unveiling of the sacred image, the song of the faithful who greet the appearance of the light—that seems to me the greatest punishment . . ."

Confronted by the voice and trembling shoulders of my mother I felt a new revulsion, difficult to resist, and in order not to see her I looked down at the mosaic on the floor. As at the first meetings with Valerian the dolphin danced among the waves, suspended in a heedless silence, the same that came now from the chair where Lucilla was sitting. Eyes down, I went back in my mind to all the years she had spent looking for solace in an imperial exception, in her husband's career, in love for a young slave, in a mad fervor, everywhere but in me, her only remaining child. Overwhelmed with bitterness, I struck her in the face. While she stared at me without a groan, obscenely enjoying that unexpected punishment, that unhoped-for suffering, I heard steps approaching from the garden. Afraid that they were announcing the arrival of my father, I fled the house of my childhood like a sinner from the temple.

Late in the night I knocked at Valerian's door. No sound came from the room, so I knocked louder, repeatedly, then called his name. Without wondering if he was absent or asleep, I slid to the floor, my back against the wall, to warm myself at the weak flame of a lamp. Weariness, arriving in waves, numbed my limbs, pushing me to the edge of sleep, where terrible visions awaited me—Daphne lying on her back in her own blood while I was still clutching the knife, Daphne struggling as I locked my hands around her throat—and every time a jolt of anguish catapulted me into wakefulness.

I don't know after how long the figure of Valerian emerged from the darkness of the garden to suddenly stand over me. I jumped to my feet, worry and suffering became frenzy, driving me to throw my arms around his neck. I wanted to ask him where he had been until that late hour, bitter reproaches burned my lips, and instead I covered his face with kisses, until he freed himself from my embrace with a gesture of irritation. He went into the room, letting one hand run along the door, as if to keep it open, and I slipped inside, along with his shadow.

As I watched him undress in silence, the impulses to flee, to attack him, to unite with him continuously replaced one another, canceling any gestures, nailing me to that spot. Perhaps he took pity on my torment, because, holding out a hand, he said, "Cecilia, come . . ."

The tone was gentle, of a casual kindness that should have invited me to prudence, but although I perceived it clearly, I wanted to exchange it for a different affection, and again I rushed to embrace him. I knew that his clasp was meant not to welcome me but to maintain a distance and contain me—entreaties and sorrowful pleas were worthless—but then I reached an unknown source, and a way opened up to me. Suddenly I sought his body with gestures I had never learned, I drew him in with words never uttered: words and gestures that said not love but a sharp passion to which Valerian yielded little by little, drawn in with bewilderment and attraction, like someone playing a game whose rules have been subverted, subverting them in turn and raising the stakes with cold sensuality. At times I recognized the gaze of his evil genius. Although on our wedding night that extraordinary apparition had distressed and frightened me, now fear and distress enjoined me to let myself go and drown, again and again, in a sea of pleasure and insult. Until dawn we struggled, one against the other, one together with the other, each with himself. Then, without a word, we separated.

I preserve a fragment of an agonizing dream, in which, after a long time, Quintus again appeared to me. I want to make note of it, surprised that, in spite of everything, the gods were willing to visit me.

Slowly the forest where I found myself was stripped of leaves, and the trunks fell to the ground, making a labyrinth of low walls that extended as far as the eye could see, while I heard the voices of Marta and Quintus, who, in the dazzling sunlight, appeared as threads of dark wool, perfectly aligned, by which to guide myself. They will lead me out of here, I thought, following in their tracks, until I realized that, every time, I returned to the point of departure. The threads continued to vibrate deceptively through the labyrinth—I was about to tear them when they enveloped me in a violent whirlwind. A moment later I found myself beside Carite, kneeling before the chapel of the family divinities. Like miniature living beings, the Lares danced around figurines of the Emperor and the august Faustina, while in the background stood a statue of Jove, from whose broad shoulders sprouted, with a strange effect, the little wings of Love. Oppressed by his immobility and his silence, I prostrated myself, entreating him to reveal himself, but the marble seemed to harden at every word and shine with an increasingly cold light, until Carite ordered me to be silent. I heard her whispering in an incomprehensible language, felt her whole being absorbed in the prayer. After a while, warmed to life, Jove the father, in the voice of Quintus, gave his response: "You must cut out her bones, and replace the liver and the heart, because she has used them up."

Entire days pass without my meeting Valerian, who is increasingly taken up by business and his duties as a magistrate. At night, however, a man and woman appear who preserve only our visible wrapping. While the bodies impose their claims, the souls withdraw into solitude and disgust. When he leaves my room I hope he won't return. Gradually as the day advances, emptied by idleness, corroded by restlessness, my only desire is to see him again. But this kind of passion is not suitable for a wife and, as soon as I am expecting his child, he will stop looking for me.

"You'll get sick like this," Carite repeats when she sees me staying in bed all day. She hesitates, she seems on the point of wanting to tell me a burning truth, but each time she retreats. Or, with an enthusiasm I've never known in her, she talks to me about sin, about my sin, and about redemption.

"If only I could save you, without this tremendous fear I have of losing you," she said yesterday, hurrying from my room.

PART THREE

Even if I knew all the languages on earth, the rhymes of the most subtle poet, the most moving harmonies, if I had the precise brushstroke of a painter, no word, no sound or color in this world would enable me to describe the light that suddenly enveloped me. I saw it, I perceived its fragrance and heard its harmony though I was dissolved in its sweet crown of fire: a light compared to which the sun would appear opaque and pale, a light that permeated soul and body, dissolving boundaries, and emanated happiness and love, peace and fulfillment.

In the comfort I got as a child from Carite's embrace, in the peace I found later in my father's, in the expansion of my soul that I sometimes discovered in music, I had had only an intuition of that grace.

As in a broken mosaic I see Carite putting a rag between my teeth so that I wouldn't bite my tongue. A doctor who was not my father wrapped me in warm cloths and performed useless fumigations.

My nurse had asked Telifrone to write to the master to come to Rome right away. But the Tiber had flooded, making Via Flaminia impassable, and the messenger had returned without discharging his duty.

So Carite, who already believed in the true God, wept and prayed for an entire day, and he answered her despair by giving her a dream in which I appeared recovered, next to a solemn, luminous man, dressed in the Greek style.

Upon waking she went to the deacon Callistus, who confirmed that Alexander, a brother from the church in Philippi, had just arrived in Rome, and to him God had granted the gift of healing by means of the Spirit.

I'm aware of the jolting of the litter, the din of the streets, the piercing cold as if they were muffled by a fog—on this interminable journey between life and death, between death and life—then the shadow and the warmth of a room and a male voice that in the name of Jesus ordered the demon to leave me.

In an instant the trembling disappeared. I see again Alexander's hand, and I who took it in mine, who left the bed cured—every nerve, every drop of blood brought to life by all that light—I a quivering little flame that rose, above the roof, toward the sky.

I barely noticed Carite, who was prostrated at Alexander's feet, thanking God.

When I returned, Valerian's house seemed strange: I still felt a wonderful sweetness, mixed with longing for my house, my true house, which I had finally found in that extraordinary moment, as at night a lost lamb finds again the arms of the shepherd. The same longing that I feel now, and that almost prevents me from holding the pen.

I questioned Carite about Jesus and she told me that she had converted to the religion of the Christians shortly after my marriage, when Theodorus told her that he had abandoned magic for a faith whose miracles were performed not by the intervention of demonic forces but by the love and power of the Lord. She had gone with him to a meeting during which a Christian had recounted some episodes of the life of the son of the only God, who died on the cross to save our souls and give us eternal life.

She who had lost her way on a thousand streets, imagining she was protecting those she loved from harm, she who had called on the aid of this or that divinity without knowing she was in error, she who was only an ignorant slave, on hearing the stories of the life of our Savior had understood with all her soul that she had found the way, the only way by which to defeat death and save us . . . How many times recently she had wanted to talk to me about Jesus—every time she had torn her hair at the sight of my despair.

While Carite, almost as upset as I, was confiding in me, I felt, more vividly than ever, her struggle between the desire to share her faith of redemption and the fear of compromising me in a religion unpopular among the people and opposed by the authorities. But I was so insistent on meeting Alexander again that in the end she agreed to talk about it with the community and, if necessary, testify in my favor.

Yesterday I waited anxiously for her return. As I waited I stammered a prayer to the unknown God who had decided to save me from death. And when I felt that the words were no use I welcomed his mystery with all the silence my soul is capable of.

Finally Carite returned and reported that, learning the names of my father and my husband, some of the faithful, among them the deacon Callistus, had given an unfavorable judgment, believing that my entrance into that church even on trial was risky. Others, however, and in particular the highest authority, the presbyter Hermas, had maintained that my status would bring honor and benefits to the community.

After a long discussion the latter view prevailed, and I have been summoned this afternoon. All the contemptuous opinions I have heard of the Christians come to mind. Atheists, enemies of Rome and the human race, according to the teacher Bebius Servianus. Frogs convened in a council in a swamp, worms assembling in a muddy hole quarreling to decide which is the guiltiest was how Ennius Severus had described them at a banquet. I remember the look my father gave him, without replying, a look obscured by concern, perhaps an unlucky presentiment.

Even if I've never heard him express an opinion about them, I'm sure that, although less offensive, it would not be kind. And yet, for the first time, I don't care what he thinks. My God, a spark of your light remains in my small, fragile soul. How I would like to pick it up in my hands, protect it, make sure it doesn't go out! And now all I want is to hurry to you.

Petronia's house, where the community meets, is on the Via Appia, but Carite preferred to go on foot because she thought it imprudent for the litter-bearers to see me return to that place.

In my heart there was only hope, and I hardly noticed the

driving rain, the difficulty of making our way through the narrow crowded streets.

Suddenly, through the half-closed curtain of a litter, I glimpsed the pale fat face of the Prefect of the Games, Portius Acilius, and I covered my face with the wet veil, in fear that he would recognize me and report it to his protégé.

Valerian! It seemed to me incredible that until that moment I hadn't given him a thought. I felt his gaze resting on my cheeks reddened by excitement, on my soaked, stained cloak, on my muddy feet, a gaze that paralyzed body and mind, preventing me from taking another step, from articulating any defense in my behalf. I don't know how long I stood still in the middle of the swirling crowd. Then I felt a hand grasp mine and heard the voice of Carite, who ordered me to start walking again.

At Petronia's house I was led into the study, where Alexander, Hermas, the deacon Callistus, and a man named Apollonius were waiting for me. In my wet and exhausted state, I hesitated to accept the invitation to sit down. Alexander took off his cloak and threw it over my shoulders. Hermas had a cup of hot water brought, urging me to drink. When it was clear that I had recovered, the presbyter asked me to repeat my name and the names of my father and husband. As I uttered them they had a distant sound, as if they belonged to unknown persons. The presbyter then questioned me about my desire to become a Christian, insistent on knowing if anyone in the family, besides Carite, knew about it or had been converted. I answered that I thought I was the only one in both families and that I hadn't talked about it with anyone. I tried to describe my physical and moral devastation, and the turmoil of my entire soul that had followed the healing performed by the brother from Philippi in the name of Jesus. In no way could I—or can I—account for such a transfiguration or say what, precisely, it consists of, but I felt that Cecilia was no longer Cecilia, I was no longer I, and at the same time I was truly I, Cecilia, finally the true Cecilia. No longer unhappy, constantly restless, unable to find peace of mind, but new, refreshed, as I had never felt before . . . Even though it was difficult to find the words and I expressed myself awkwardly, the presbyter nodded kindly. When Apollonius interrupted to assess my knowledge of the doctrine, I couldn't do more than repeat the rudiments I had learned from my nurse.

Hermas reasserted the existence of a single God, creator of the universe, of all things visible and invisible, and of Christ, his son, the Savior, foretold by the prophets. He spoke of a way of Life that I will have to follow from now on, and a way of Death that I must abandon, casting aside mute delusive idols. He asked me if I was ready to renounce them, the first step in confessing the new faith. Partly hiding the truth, I answered that it was a long time since I had addressed to them either prayers or offerings.

After an exchange of glances the four men withdrew, leaving me alone in the room.

While I waited for their answer the possibility of not being accepted took on more precise and distressing outlines. I recalled the apprehension I had felt during the midwife's visit, my fear of being considered unworthy to marry Valerian. A laughable fear, compared to what I felt now.

Yes, Hermas spoke the truth when he evoked two opposite ways, and for a moment I seemed to see them open up before me—one an easy downhill slope, the other steep and arduous, each so different from the goal it led to. I found myself at the crossroads, or, rather, if I thought about it carefully, on the edge of a precipice, since at that moment life or death depended not on me but on their decision. My God, make them accept me, do not abandon me now! If they reject me I will fall back into despair, because I'm afraid that alone, far from Alexander, who saved me, and without the help of the community, I will lose you again.

When, finally, they returned, the presbyter declared that if I demonstrated the will to behave in an exemplary manner I would be accepted into the church to learn the principal elements of the doctrine. With the gratitude one can feel only for those who give us life or restore it to us, I embraced them one after the other, but if my impulse was identical toward all, their enthusiasm was not. The clasp of the presbyter was paternal and serious, equally fraternal was that of Alexander (no man ever embraced me like that), Apollonius smiled at me, while Callistus seemed cold and insincere.

Returning home, I rejoiced with all my heart that I did not see my husband, and even more when I realized that the cause of that joy was not the fear of being seen on the crowded streets of an obscure neighborhood but the sudden absence of every hope in regard to him.

I didn't know how to pray: in my room I knelt and thanked God for that first sign of change in me. In a low voice I sang a song free of every formula, taking words and sounds that arose spontaneously on my lips: a hymn to Jesus, proclaimed by prophets I knew nothing about.

I leave a blank space to indicate a pause. Ridiculous stratagem! To write, when I wish only to pray—I would like to be only prayer. Or to write to you, my God, a few lines every morning of a long letter to tell you how much I miss you. In the moment of my recovery, you were in me, alive and real, and I in you, I felt your presence in my entire, restored body, while suffering was dissolved in the certainty of your love.

But what words to use now? New letters would be useful, new signs. Not Latin or Greek: it's the language of angels I would like to speak. A language like feathers, like embroidery.

Lord, only you can inspire that in your creature. And since I am not an angel, dictate to me the words with which to express, along with the joy, the hunger and thirst for your love.

Simple words to express the vastness of Heaven, words like brushstrokes of color to express the beauty of your creation. The heart can hold them, now that my house is a step from Heaven. This morning, on waking, I went into the garden. There were just a few clouds, as if sketched by the tips of the cypresses waving in the light breeze. A blackbird whistled, while at my feet a parade of ants headed industriously toward their nest. In an instant everything appeared to me in your perfection. I am seeing the world for the first time.

The majority of my brothers are slaves, poor people, foreigners. I used to pass them on the street without seeing them. They didn't exist for the blind eyes of my heart. Now those strangers have become my brothers in Christ: men and women of flesh and blood, who for a long time appeared to me only as ghosts.

They don't know how to read or write, their clothes are threadbare, their breath is heavy with garlic, and yet I feel close to them in a way I've felt only with Annia. Every day I know them a little better, and I find them interesting, an entire world to discover. It's a curiosity I never felt about the friends of my father and my husband, always rigorously behind their masks, without surprises. Or about the guests at our banquets, ready to share only with those who are not in need, only with those who are currently in power. My brothers share everything.

Perpetua is a widow who survives on aid from the community. Possessing nothing, not even a roof to shelter her, she was welcomed into Petronia's house. She has many ailments, and yet I've never met anyone more cheerful, more heedless of her own sufferings. She limps, and has a hard time getting around, while her deep laugh echoes through the rooms.

Prisca is a young slave. She is barely thirteen, slender and white as a lily of the valley. In spite of that, every day she finds the courage to secretly leave the house of her masters and come to the community to take part in the prayers or readings. And I am always moved by her concentrated, serious expression as she tries to follow Hermas through the forest of Books. She who has never seen a book in her life.

Apollonius is the son of rich Syrian merchants. He knew my father among the Stoics and says he has great respect for him. They are about the same age, and resemble each other not only in their features but also in their habits. Behind a simple, mild manner, Apollonius conceals an uncommon knowledge: before finding the Way in the school of Justin Martyr he tried many philosophical sects, but was always disappointed in the truths they claimed to offer.

Callistus, the deacon, is an educated freedman. His knowing gaze gives the impression that he is aware of everything about our little community, perhaps even what the brothers do not say. In good works he is tireless: after two hours of sleep he is already going through the city distributing gifts to the needy.

How to describe the admiration I feel for Petronia? She welcomes us in her house, strips herself of her wealth to give it to widows and the poor, helps the deacon take care of orphans, tends sick women, informs the presbyter about everyone's needs. In her presence I understand that if prayer is words, the word is not a dead letter but life and love. She was a rich matron, and now she has calluses on her hands from so much work and blisters on her feet from all the miles she walks to visit the needy.

Yesterday, for the first time, I went with her to a part of Rome, not far from the Via Appia, that I didn't know existed. At the back of a sort of cave, I made out a vaguely human figure lying on a pile of straw, and I followed Petronia, who, going up to her, told me, "Her name is Chia, and she's very ill and has no one to take care of her."

Before my eyes a deformed body materialized, the limbs swollen like goatskins. Veins and capillaries appeared on her translucent skin: a pattern of pulsing rivulets of red blood and blue, always on the point of breaking through. Recognizing

Petronia the girl raised her head, gazing at her with such hope that it filled me with pity and distress—fear that her skin would burst, and she would be bathed in blood, like Quintus. I had the impulse to close my eyes, to flee, and yet I managed to carry out calmly the orders that Petronia gave me. I brought water from the fountain and helped wash Chia's body. As I held her in my arms I felt that I was in yours, my God. And I felt that I could, yes, now I can love myself and love my neighbor.

I think back to the days when I didn't know what to do with myself. The boredom, the diffidence. My God, I thank you for revealing to me not only Heaven but earth, an earth that I seem to possess whole, with overwhelming joy, now that it is no longer confined by the walls of houses and splendid villas, now that I am walking toward Heaven. Thank you for not forgetting me, for not abandoning me in that gilded desperation, in tormented questions that have no answers and sins that cannot be expiated. Carite gave me her milk. Carite led me to your fountain. The soul of Annia, omen of your eternity. Quintus, dark sorrow, the substitute's death and then the thread that led me to you. Valerian, yes also Valerian, the blow that wounded me. My God, how many threads in the fabric you destined for me alone. Thank you for having called me to live for you, to act for you, to love and serve my brothers who suffer.

Today, during the reading, I felt the eyes of Prassede, a young freedwoman, resting for a long time on my gold bracelet. A silent, urgent request that led me later to give it to her. It was the last piece of jewelry I had left, a gift from my parents: the rest I had already sold to give alms to the presbytery.

With his business and with the position of questor, which gives him access to the treasury of Rome, Valerian is daily increasing his own wealth.

While the house on the Palatine is decorated with valuable works of art, I no longer buy silks or jewels or books.

The money for household expenses has become a huge sum, but how I regret the time when I didn't know what use to make of it! Now I don't dare to draw on it to provide money for the church. I'm too afraid that Valerian would notice. There, I've just written his name, and the peace that reigned in my soul until a moment ago has disappeared. Yes, I'm still afraid of him. Is the old Cecilia not dead and buried after all?

For hours I prayed to find the strength to overcome my reticence and pride so that, at the urging of Hermas, yesterday I was able to confess my sins in front of the assembly. Many brothers and sisters were present and, as I entered the room, I was afraid that what I was preparing to say would arouse their hatred.

I stood up, hesitant, as they observed me expectantly, but suddenly I felt your love—and was again serene and trusting. And, feeling neither humiliation nor shame, I spoke sincerely about my mistakes. Even when I admitted the most terrible things—that I had enjoyed seeing a slave bleed under the kicks of her mistress, had imagined, out of jealousy, strangling my maid, had even caused the death of a young slave with my wealthy girl's weakness and pride—my voice was firm, as if the one who had committed those sins had been not me but another woman who no longer existed.

Hermas urged me to give proof of repentance by giving alms and fasting, Monica knelt and entreated me to forgive the envy she feels toward me, Felix praised my sincerity and my willingness to improve myself.

But it's strange: sometimes I feel like a newborn, sometimes old and feeble, weighed down by sins and failings . . . Courage! How many steps await me still on the Way.

This morning I wrote a letter to my mother, asking her forgiveness for having often judged her and, in my heart, condemned her. For having dared to reproach her when she was lost in confusion and despair.

Then I went to find Daphne in the slaves' rooms and confessed that I had imagined killing her. She looked at me with incredulity and fear, then she made as if to flee but I held her by the hem of her tunic and knelt before her and kissed her feet. She was all trembling, and wept. I had to talk to her for a long time to calm her and convince her that I no longer wish her harm.

For the first time I visited Chia by myself. On the way to her cave, in spite of all the noise and fumes of the crowded streets, I heard only birdsong and caught the scent of thaw: of spring spreading a carpet of flowers at my feet. I felt that I was shining, a point of radiant light. I looked at the passersby, the people at work, even the harsh schoolmaster, and I bathed them in that light, that love, hoping that my eyes could speak.

When I entered Chia's cave she seemed disappointed not to see Petronia, and in a whisper asked why she hadn't come. But I felt strong, capable of doing anything for her. Her skin no longer upset me, I felt neither fear nor disgust as I washed her body with a damp cloth. And I who don't know how to do a single thing, not even how to mend a tiny tear in my *stola*, washed her blanket at the fountain, and then brought food, and fed her. Slowly I felt that she trusted my gestures, and at one point she smiled at me. The most wonderful gift I've ever had.

Last night the Lord gave me this vision. I found myself with Quintus, Marta, and a little girl I didn't know in the shade of a great oak. Like calves, we were drinking the milk that dripped from our mothers' breasts. It tasted like honey and filled us with delight. Then the girl smiled at me, embraced me, and finally I smelled again the odor of my sister.

My Annia, the cruel flower-shaped wound had disappeared

from your forehead, and now I know that you are happy where you are. There are soft fields there and you can run barefoot. There are kind souls, who rock you in their soft moth wings. I don't want to disturb you anymore, take you away from your peace, turning to you at every moment . . . Annia, you see me, you know me, you know that I have never stopped loving you.

I continue to avoid Valerian, the mere sight of whom fills me with revulsion and fear.

Hermas, when I told him this, urged me to be upright and modest in relation to him, for it sometimes happens that a non-believer husband is converted thanks to a believing wife. I said nothing, staring at him doubtfully, and he understood: he advised me to be prudent and, without falling into sin, obey him.

Even last night, when he knocked at the door calling my name, I hid my head under the covers in order not to hear him. Finally, forced to let him in, I stifled my repulsion toward his body and the servitude of mine, and pretended tenderness. He examined me as if in search of a secret, then said he found me changed and strange. "What's happening to you? You didn't seem to dislike it so much before . . ." he whispered, as I burned with shame.

Distant, indifferent, Valerian reads my soul with an ease that humiliates me, rekindling refusal and rebellion. Every time, I put him off with a pretext until I remember the presbyter's advice and again cover his face with lying kisses.

I am compelled to utter other lies to conceal from him how often I go out to Petronia's house.

The hours devoted to learning have increased since Apollonius, in order to answer the questions with which I interrupt the reading of the Books, said he was willing to study in more depth certain aspects of the doctrine with me.

Together we began to reread the books of the Jewish prophets, who accurately foresaw events of the future, anticipating the coming of Jesus, his death and resurrection.

Apollonius reads, then responds patiently to all my questions, or interprets the passages that seem obscure to me. But how often his explanations leave me confused and discouraged. I don't understand the language of God! The mysterious images that envelop you, as if you were hiding. With thought I'll never succeed. Rather, abandon myself, listen . . . I find you, friend and neighbor, within me, in your embrace, when I sing the Psalms.

I've transcribed them, one by one, and I play on the zither as I sing.

As I used to do when my mother was pregnant, I shut myself in a secluded room to play, far from indiscreet ears, when I'm sure that Valerian isn't home. The song of those simple yet powerful lines, whispers and cries, sighs and laughter that adapt themselves so well to the most diverse moments, erases your inaccessibility. In the emotion of the music, while you hold me in your great hand, I am nothing but your instrument. My God, give me a perfect ear so that, amid the tumult of the world, I can hear the silence that shows me the Way.

But how can I tell Apollonius that I've already heard enough explanations? He would say that I am in error, in sin. And that I will be saved only if I accept the Word.

My God, what use to me are the Books if I don't have your love?

I remember all the times I pressed Hermas to shorten the waiting period, and how I insisted when he pointed out that, although there was no doubt of my fervor, it was still too soon for me to have learned the doctrine and be able to follow its precepts.

Finally, three days ago, Alexander and Apollonius gave a favorable opinion, but now that a few hours separate me from baptism I can't sleep; maybe fasting has added to my restlessness. One moment I find myself at the culmination of hope, the next tears of despair bathe my face.

I woke my nurse and, in her arms, said I wasn't ready for this serious step, didn't feel strong or worthy enough to sustain such grace. She repeated that it is baptism itself that bestows worth and purity, because it's a miracle that will instantaneously wash away my sins: I will be immersed in the blood of Christ, will die with him, and with him be reborn.

There are those among us who claim that a second chance should not be granted and that, after baptism, neither confession nor penitence avails. What will become of me? Even though I feel that I'm better, I fear the obstinacy of evil, of my wicked nature . . .

And yet Hermas must consider me ready, since he didn't make me wait three years. Apollonius is never tired of repeating these words: I who was born without an act of my will, ignorant of my primal origin, from liquid seed through the union of my parents, and who lived amid evil customs and unjust habits, I, through baptism, which is enlightenment, will go from being a daughter of destiny and ignorance to being a daughter of free will and knowledge, and will obtain the remission of sins committed. Didn't the Lord say, "And if your sins are like purple, I will make them white as wool, and if they are like scarlet, I will make them white as snow"?

How much I want to believe Carite, Hermas, and Apollonius at this precise instant, as dawn lightens my room, after a night of weeping and praying.

Lord, I am again in darkness! If at least the darkness would hide me from your gaze! Or if I could emerge from it, as in the moment of my recovery, rise up in a single moment in all that light, feel again the warmth of your embrace. But meanwhile the way of Life and the way of Death seem constantly intertwined, I confuse one with the other, I confuse the precepts of Hermas with those of Pallante, the teachings of my father with those of Apollonius, while the words of the prophets seem to me indecipherable enigmas. Trying to calm down, I transcribe a psalm, singing it in a whisper:

"My soul awaits the Lord
More eagerly than the sentinels the dawn . . ."

With Hermas leading me by the hand, I stepped into the fountain in the garden.

Insensible to the bite of the cold, I was immersed up to my head, and he bathed it, baptizing me in the name of the Father, the Son, and the Holy Ghost.

On my face tears of gratitude mingled with the water of the fountain. Was it the salt of tears that I tasted in my mouth, or of the blood of Jesus? The blood of Jesus that flowed together with my poor blood? And the sweet taste that tempered its bitterness—was it the water of liberation and salvation? Meanwhile, serenity filled my heart like a quiet lake, rising again and again, to overflow, enveloping me, protecting me, like the cloak that the presbyter threw over my shoulders to protect me from the cold.

With a step that in all my life was never so firm, I followed him into the room where the Eucharist took place, and from which until now I had been excluded. I crossed the threshold without hesitation. Waiting for me were many brothers and sisters—Callistus and Felix, Monica and Isidorus, Perpetua, Prisca, Avilius, Origene, Saturninus, Faustus, and Priscilla, Hermas's wife—and soon I was surrounded by Carite's joy, Petronia's smile, the encouraging gaze of Apollonius, Alexander's serious one. Together they sang a hymn to Christ, then they all embraced me and kissed one another. The deacon Callistus brought Hermas bread and a chalice of water and wine. And raising the chalice the presbyter said, "We give thanks, O our Father, for the holy life of your David, whom you showed us by means of Jesus, your servant. Glory to you forever."

Breaking the bread, he said, "We thank you, O our Father, for the knowledge and the life that you have pointed out to us through Jesus, your servant. Glory to you forever."

While I ate the body of Christ and drank his blood, I felt that my body was losing its mortal nature, that it was saturated with immortality. I thought of Annia, of how I wrote to her in the hope that she might hear and understand me, of her child's odor in the vision God sent me, and suddenly I knew that I would find her again, after the Judgment Day, and that, identical in body and soul, we would recognize each other.

At the end of the Eucharist we addressed a prayer of thanks to the Lord, ending with these words:

"May grace arrive and may this world pass. Hosanna to the God of David! Let those who are without sin go forward; let those who are not repent. The Lord is coming. So be it."

In the quiet of the gathering Alexander's voice rose; to him, as to every saint, we are allowed to give thanks with our own prayers. I had learned that the Spirit descended upon him, bestowing not only the gift of healing but also that of speaking in tongues. When I heard him utter incomprehensible words, each phrase drawn perhaps from Aramaic, from Hebrew, from Sanskrit—or from languages unknown to men—I began to tremble in fear and wonder and I closed my eyes.

Gradually, in the darkness, I noticed an even more astonishing fact: those indecipherable sounds, so different from one another, melded into a poignant melody, both prayer and praise, in which I felt the ardor of a unique faith, the power of a unique Spirit. And suddenly, while Alexander went on praying, I heard only silence and, in it, the voice of God.

The awe that the apostle from Philippi inspired in me has disappeared, and now his friendship seems to me more precious than that of Hermas or Apollonius. He never speaks of himself, but his rare words, even the simplest, are so remarkable that sometimes they are enough to satisfy my thirst for God, whereas sometimes they intensify it, turning it almost into a cry. Maybe it's because grace never abandons him, while the Lord at times hides within me, like a spring buried by rocks and sand that I am unable to unearth. Yesterday I felt like a thirsty person digging in the ground, and when I confessed this to Alexander he urged me to pray with my own words. Hands raised, I prayed in silence, in my soul: my God, take me by the hand, so I may go through the world like a wanderer, and perhaps I will be able to radiate a spark of your light, a little of the love that you harbor for your children. Take me by the hand and I will live, bluebells and cornflowers will sprout from my fingertips.

I was about to go to sleep when I remembered all the letters I've received from Lucretia, and one from Domitilla, which I hadn't had time or inclination to open. With a jolt of loyalty I made an effort to get up, and light the lamp.

Domitilla tells me that she is pregnant and gives me news of her life in Mantua, where her husband, Sextus Cinna, was transferred as prefect, thanks to the intervention of Valerian. Of Lucretia's letters, which I skimmed rapidly, I want to transcribe one, because it painfully, eloquently illustrates the distance that now separates me from my dearest friend:

My Cecilia,
You won't answer me. I tell you I'm coming to see you, and don't find you at home. I show up without warning two days in a row, and Benedetta tells me that you have gone out. Are you avoiding me? Have I offended you in some way, without realizing it? Or maybe . . . but yes, of course, what a fool not to have thought of it before . . . Surely for you, too, the moment

has arrived to discover the delights of a non-marital embrace! But it's unfair . . . to conceal it from someone who has never had secrets from you . . .

My dear, poor Lucretia!

Tormented, filled with uncertainty, I couldn't sleep all that night thinking of her.

I reproached myself for having kept this new happiness to myself, so early in the morning I went to see her. But it was pointless.

I hoped with all my heart that Lucretia would understand me, I prayed to God that she would understand when I told her about my miraculous cure, about Alexander, who saved me from death in the name of Jesus, and that now I spent my time among the Christians.

"You frighten me," she broke in, as soon as she heard the word. "I don't know them, but I know how they end up. They're sent to die in the arenas or hanged on a cross."

I told her that thus was fulfilled the sacrifice of Jesus, the son of God, who died on the cross to wash away our sins and give us eternal life . . .

She stopped me again, insisting that she didn't want to hear anything about it. Rather, she was adamant that I should forget about them. And she asked me to promise that I wouldn't go back to the community.

She held me tight, continuing to insist, sadness in her voice. When I was silent, she pushed me away: "You're as impulsive as ever, stubborn as ever . . . Promise me at least that you'll be careful."

And while an unbearable inertia prevented me from speaking, stifling every temptation to try to persuade her, all I could do was nod, miserable and defeated.

Later I confided to Alexander that my faith is weak, that I was unable to speak to Jesus, that I didn't even have the power to make myself heard by my best friend. I also told him that, in spite of the baptism, the old Cecilia, with all her flaws, her laziness, her diffidence, still controls me like an evil demon. Then I feel again the full weight of my sins.

"What is unquiet here," and Alexander indicated my head, "must find repose here," and he indicated the heart. "You think too much, Cecilia. Instead you must welcome into your heart the mystery of God. You must pray for the young slave, and continue to listen."

I prayed all night until the Lord gave me the grace of a vision in which Quintus appeared, sitting serenely under the majestic oak with his sister, and I went to them without fear.

I think of Pallante, of the emptiness of his beautiful, complex speeches. Alexander sees into the depths of my soul. With simple yet inspiring words, he touches me to the core. He is so full of love, faith, and strength that when I find him with someone else I feel lost. My God, it's true, I want his love to be all for me.

s the round stone cannot become square unless it is cut and loses a part of itself, so those who are rich in this world, if their wealth is not diminished, cannot become useful to the Lord. So you, when you were rich, were useless; now, however, you are useful and ready for life." And this morning, after reading that passage of the Good Shepherd, Callistus raised an accusatory glance at me: he wants my money and that's why he hates me.

If some of the brethren remind me of the weight of my fortune with explicit requests, Hermas continues to urge that, like all the well-off Christians in Rome, I give for the benefit of the poorer communities in the provinces.

Some days ago I wrote a letter to my father, asking him for twenty thousand sesterces without telling him why. His answer had a tone of concern: was Valerian not providing for my needs? A few hours later, though, another messenger brought me the sum, accompanied by these brief words: "I obey my little lady."

I gave the money to the presbyter: half will remain in our treasury, the other half will be sent to the Churches of Jerusalem and Antioch.

And yet, since it seems to me that I never give enough, I am constantly worrying. What was once part of me like a quality of nature, the color of my eyes or hair, now seems to me a monstrous excrescence that has to be cut out of my body.

Petronia, to whom I unburden myself, comparing the joy

and naturalness of her generosity with mine, which is always troubled and not spontaneous, reassures me. She, too, at first perceived her fortune as a blot, inspiring in the brothers sometimes condemnation, sometimes adulation. She used to come to the assembly in her usual brilliant robes, and someone would always offer her the most comfortable seat or, on the contrary, would look at her with hostility or envy. Giving up every exterior sign of wealth had been the first step, yet it was not sufficient to make her comfortable. Then, when she began to offer donations at every worship, she put her offerings in the hands of Hermas, who consecrated them on the altar.

But one night Jesus appeared to her in a dream, surrounded by the disciples, and when she asked him what good work she must do to obtain eternal life, he answered, as in the encounter with the wealthy young man in the Gospel of Matthew, that she was to observe the commandments and, if she wanted to be perfect, sell all that she possessed, give it to the poor, and follow him. Unlike the wealthy young man, Petronia welcomed with happiness the exhortation of Jesus, who said to his disciples: "In truth I say to you: to God all is possible, even that a camel should pass through the eye of a needle."

That deliberate gesture gradually became simpler, and her prodigality, like a natural fountain that seems to revive each time one approaches, began to flow inexhaustibly. It seems to her that she is thus offering a magnificent spectacle not to the world but to Heaven, not to an emperor or a consul but to God and all the angels.

Besides, Petronia says, continuing to reassure me, she is a widow, without children, and this makes her free. While I must still account to my husband for every step, word, and action. If anything, it is I who should be admired, and she advises me to persevere.

Today, with trembling hands, for the first time I took five thousand sesterces from Valerian's funds. *With trembling hands.*

My God, why am I still so afraid of him, when every day I feel your strength growing in my heart?

S ome of the brothers are beginning to look unkindly on Alexander's stay in the community.

This morning, during the meeting, Felix said openly, "I live on your charity, because I stopped sculpting and painting idols, and, not knowing how to do anything else, I can't find work. But Alexander? The Didache states that every apostle must be welcomed like the Lord, but that he can stay in the community only for a day, at most two, if it's really necessary. If he stays for three days without work he is a false prophet."

An uproar arose: some agreed, others were indignant at his insinuations. Hermas intervened to calm everyone down, reproaching Felix and defending Alexander: has he not always lived in poverty, demonstrating that he is not abusing our welcome? Not to mention that, unlike a false prophet, the brother from Philippi does not confine himself to teaching the truth but takes care to practice it.

The presbyter then reminded everyone of the virtue of hospitality toward strangers, and the exhortations of the apostle Paul on that subject, a virtue that the Roman community practiced from its beginnings, aware that, precisely because of its location in the capital of the Empire, it had to take an active role in tending to the practical needs of the Church of Christ.

Now silence reigned, but as soon as the presbyter adjourned the meeting the murmuring started up again, this time against Felix. I couldn't hear what the brothers had to say because Hermas called me aside.

"Cecilia, I've noticed that for some time you've been shirking the duty of going with Petronia to help the needy, in order to remain in Alexander's company. I see no harm in the fact that you find in him instruction and repose, because, as I've said, he is a holy man. In spite of that, in your case it worries me. To feel in any way the presence of God is a great gift, but it's not everything, and is not reserved for everyone. From your words, from the way you behave in Alexander's presence, I see that you consider charisms the supreme good, that you aspire to them more than to do the will of our Lord, which is that we devote ourselves to his works, for our neighbor and for ourselves, converting every day, following the way of Life and abandoning the way of Death. Your woman's sensibility, your frailty, combined with the circumstance of having received an education rare for a woman, incline you to prefer spiritual fervor at the expense of discipline, the expectation of a vision at the expense of exercising vigilance, solitary communion with God to speaking with men by example. Such an attitude, my daughter, does not make you useful to the community and risks leading to lack of respect and pride."

I bowed my head, feeling these warnings like a lash, and did not say a word.

Even though it depends not on my intention but on my not daring to touch Valerian's money, it's true that recently I've been less generous with donations and more reluctant to give. It's true that, in order to not be distant from Alexander, from the grace that he seems to instill in me, I've neglected Petronia and helping the poor and the sick.

Out of fear of being judged arrogant, I confessed only to him the visions of blessedness and the dream with which God answered my prayers. That Alexander can unveil every thought, every impulse of my soul no longer surprises me. But can Hermas read so deeply into my heart, he who seems to be occupied solely with the practical responsibilities of the church, with discipline, and with giving the clearest possible lessons without worrying about either the nature or the culture of those in his presence?

As I crossed the atrium to leave the house, still disturbed by the presbyter's rebuke, I paused beside Felix, who was busy painting on a wall. I observed the simple, almost childlike lines that took shape under his brush, representing a shepherd musician wearing on his head Orpheus's Phrygian cap, and surrounded by lambs and doves.

"It's you," he said, turning toward me. "You see, I can't paint anymore. I used to be very good. I painted and sculpted many idols—may God forgive me—and my art was prized. But now that I'm trying to evoke our Savior, the Lord punishes me by depriving me of all skill and refinement . . . Maybe he doesn't like them, or maybe he's punishing me for having sinned in word and deed against a brother. But there was some truth in what I said. I've given up everything in the name of Christ. Not like those who work in the temples of the idolaters in the morning and gather at night in the house of God. Not like Saturninus, who's still a schoolmaster, teaching children tales filled with the names and deeds of the dead gods, and who gives Minerva the fee paid by each new student. And not like the slaves, who have everything to gain and nothing to lose by joining us. I've even given up spectacles, which were my passion, the only diversion in a life of hard work. And now that I go hungry, and my wife and children go hungry, the spectacle that's offered is a sponger who not only blathers a lot of nonsense but has the impudence to declare that Christians should not fear hunger . . . By Hercules, the only one who has the courage to denounce him is me, and I'm rebuked for it!"

In spite of the injustice of his words, I felt sorry for him, for his sorrowful tone, the genuine sadness that issued from his impotent hand, from his body as it knelt before the awkward figure of the shepherd.

"Felix," I said, "you complain because your drawing looks like a child's, but maybe it's not a punishment, maybe it's a reward, a gift from God. Didn't Jesus say, 'If you do not become like little children, you will not enter the Kingdom of Heaven. Therefore whoever becomes little like this child will be the greatest in the Kingdom of Heaven'?"

"You are rich, Cecilia, and you are also good, may God bless you."

"But you're wrong about Alexander and the slaves," I resumed. "Without him I would be dead, in soul and body. He's not a charlatan, and never asked for money through his charisms. As for the slaves, do you really believe that Carite has nothing to lose? She lives with me not like a servant but like a mother, and I love her as I do my mother."

"Carite . . . But all the others . . . You are noble and rich, I am humble and poor, but we are both citizens. They are things, mere tools endowed with a voice. And now, thanks to this life of theirs, which is worth nothing, in the Kingdom of Heaven they will be among the most exalted, along with the children."

As soon as he had uttered these words, prostrating himself in front of the image of the shepherd, Felix began to moan: "Merciful God, have pity on my distrust, my envy, and my bitterness. Deliver me from evil, deliver me from temptation and sadness as you delivered Noah from the flood, Daniel from the lion's jaws, Jonah from the sea monster . . ."

We were waiting for the reading when the presbyter entered, ordering us to go into the garden immediately.

His face was dark, just like an irate father, and we followed him in silence to the peristyle, exchanging anxious, questioning glances.

Outside, the deacon Callistus was feeding a big fire with wood and brush, and Hermas ordered us to gather around it.

In a tone I had never heard, barely containing his anger, he scrutinized us, one by one, and said, "I have assembled you here to receive the confession of a sister who has committed grave sins. May her repentance be an example to you, because God knows all and sees all, and what you do not confess in the gathering you will be indebted for on Judgment Day." Then, in a louder voice, he declared, "Carite, you may come."

In all the confusion, I hadn't noticed her absence, and now I saw her come out of the house and approach, red in the face and with unsteady steps. From her sweat-drenched forehead, from the fists clenched at her sides, from the tremor of her lips came an anguish that immediately rekindled mine for the accusations the presbyter had made against me. In addition, exposed to public censure—something that had never happened to her even with my father, who if he had to reprimand her always did so in private—she seemed for the first time defenseless and extraordinarily in need of my help. Unable to restrain myself, I rushed to embrace her, which made things worse, because Carite burst into sobs.

I stood there, with my head hidden in her breast, until, at a call from the presbyter, she pushed me away. Then I joined the others, without the courage to look again at my nurse, who, in a low and almost unintelligible voice, continually breaking off, began her confession:

"Brothers . . . I . . . Brothers, I realize only today the seriousness . . . of the power of Evil . . . and I want, sincerely, with a pure heart, I who have sinned, I want . . . also for you . . . That you may know, that you may avoid my sin . . . In other words, I want to tell you a tremendous vision, which I have already reported to Hermas."

As her voice became gradually more serene I looked up. After a deep breath, Carite resumed:

"Some nights ago, in a dream, I saw the angels of God gathered around his dazzling light. Although I didn't understand his words, I knew that he was entrusting them with the guardianship of men and the heavenly elements. When all the angels received their commands, they flew away: some on high, disappearing from my sight, some toward the earth, at times obscuring the sun with their immense wings. But soon I saw that the serpent was wrapping them in his coils, and that the angels were beginning to look with longing at the things of the earth. They looked at women and found them beautiful. They approached with flattering words, and as soon as they coupled with them the women produced monstrous creatures, demons who, without wasting any time, took possession of human beings. Threatened by one of them I tried to flee, but in vain, because the demon enslaved me by casting a spell, then forced me to offer sacrifices and incense and libations. The most frightening thing was that, in the course of this vision, the demons assumed precise shapes and, from formless shadows, were transformed into idols, Jove, Mars, Minerva. The one that possessed me took on the features of Hecate. In obeying its will, I found myself in no time with a knot of vipers in my hair, just like a witch, practicing black magic on a murdered child. I was scraping the marrow and the shriveled liver from the little corpse in order to prepare a love potion when a powerful hand grabbed me by the throat, hurling me into the Inferno. Then I found myself in a boiling well, suffocated by a dense, stinking smoke, with a multitude who in life had practiced the demonic arts. Farther on I saw vain women hanging from trees by their hair, and lustful men hanging by their genitals, disobedient slaves who bit their tongues without respite, and usurers sunk in their own excrement. Brothers, I woke in a sea of sweat, gasping with anguish and terror. Prostrating myself on the ground, I entreated divine pardon for having consulted sorcerers and astrologers all my life, and for the fact that I still possess and use magic potions. But here before you, all our holy church, confessing my idolatry, I renounce forever the serpent's snares."

From a purse tied to her waist, Carite took some vials containing liquids of various colors and threw them into the fire. Immediately afterward, holding tight to each other to give themselves courage, Isidor and Monica approached: he tore a talisman from his neck and threw it on the fire. His wife did the same with an engraved tablet and a small vial. The flames shot up, hissing and crackling, filling many of the brothers with awe, and they knelt, begging for God's mercy.

Shaken by the force of evil evoked by Carite's vision, and at the same time by the violence of that public confession imposed on a person who could do only good, I gazed, immobilized, at the brothers, who now followed the presbyter toward the house. After I don't know how long Felix, on Hermas's orders, came to look for me in the garden. Anger creased his forehead, fury continued to vibrate in his voice, when he began reading a letter from the Church of Gaul from three years earlier:

The servants of Christ who are pilgrims in Vienna and in Lyons, in Gaul, to their brothers in Asia and Phrygia who have our faith and hope in redemption: peace, thanks, and glory from God the Father and Jesus Christ our Lord. We are unable to report in a satisfactory way on the current brutality of persecution, the anger of the pagans against the holy, and how much suffering the martyrs have endured. The Adversary has attacked with all his power, presaging what the future will be, and has resorted to every means, preparing and training his men against the servants of God, so that not only are we driven out of our houses, the baths, and the forum, but we are absolutely forbidden to appear in any public place. In spite of that, the grace of God has fought in our defense and has pushed aside the weak and fortified the strong. In the first place our brothers and sisters have courageously endured the innumerable abuses inflicted by the crowd: they have been insulted, beaten, dragged on the ground, robbed, stoned; in short they have undergone all those persecutions that an angry crowd customarily inflicts on those it considers enemies. Then, led into the forum before the tribune and the magistrates of the city and interrogated in front of all the people, they proclaimed their faith and were shut in prison until the arrival of the governor. Later, when this man was practicing every form of cruelty against them, Vettius Epagathus intervened, one whose way of life was so perfect that, in spite of his youth, it merited comparison with that of the priest Zachariah. Finding it unbearable that charges so absurd should be brought, he demanded to be heard in our defense, to show that among us there is neither atheism nor impiety. At this point the governor asked if he himself was a Christian. And, having proclaimed his faith, Vettius, too, was raised up to the fate of martyrs. Then among the remaining Christians a division occurred: some were ready to bear witness to their faith, which they did with great fervor; others, instead, appeared unprepared, still weak and unable to sustain the burden of a great struggle. Among the latter a dozen were absent from confession, causing us great sorrow and diminishing the courage of the brothers who had not yet been arrested. Meanwhile, the most eminent Christians were arrested along with some of our slaves, since the governor had publicly ordered that all should be sought. These, entrapped by Satan and fearing torture, falsely accused us of celebrating Thyestean banquets and Oedipal marriages, and of deeds that are unlawful to speak or think of or even to believe that they were ever practiced by men. Gradually as these rumors spread people grew angry against us, and became violently hostile. Thus was fulfilled the prophecy of our Lord: "The time will come when he who kills you will believe that he is worshipping God." All the wrath of the populace and of the governor and his soldiers was concentrated on Sanctus, the deacon from Vienna, on Maturus, recently baptized but a brave fighter, on Attalus, a native of Pergamus, who had been the mainstay of his people, and on Blandina, through whom Christ showed that what appears of little value, obscure, and despicable in the eyes of men is of great glory in the sight of God. In fact, while all of us, including her mistress, feared that because of the weakness of her body Blandina would not be able to confess her faith, she was sustained by such power that she exhausted those who, one after another, took turns torturing her in every manner from morning to night. Not knowing what else to do to her, marveling that she was still alive although her whole body had been racked, they had to admit defeat. But Blandina drew strength from her confession, and her comfort and relief from suffering was in exclaiming, "I am a Christian and we do nothing vile . . ."

Yesterday, for the first time, I returned home in the middle of the night. I was about to close the door of my room when I felt something in the way. Glimpsing in the semidarkness a male figure, I was afraid it was my husband. Instead, blocking the door with one foot was Telifrone, who insisted that I let him enter, with the tone of reproof that I know well.

I lighted a lamp, whose flame dug deep shadows in his face, throwing into relief its pallor and thinness, while his shoulders stuck out sharply under his *pallium*.

According to Carite, my pedagogue lately has been staying shut in his room all day reading, praying, fasting. Thus the rare times that I'm at home we never meet. Worried at seeing him so worn down, I asked if he felt ill.

"You would do better to take care of your own health, Cecilia," he answered bitterly. "Can you tell me where you were until now?"

"You forget that I'm not a child anymore," I replied, pretending lightness.

"You always think you can get away with it . . . But I know you better than myself."

The voice that marked the rhythm of gymnastic exercises or declaimed Homer, the hand that taught me to hold the plectrum and took mine as we walked under the porticos . . . I felt a pang as all the years we had spent together flashed through my mind.

I bowed my head without answering.

"The master has written to inquire about you. He is worried. He says that you no longer give him news, and when you condescend to do so you have a vague and distant tone that he doesn't recognize. Above all, you ask him for money without explaining the need. What are you doing, Cecilia?"

Even more uneasy at hearing him name my father, and conscious of having no other way out, I replied boldly, "All right, then. Since you insist. But don't dare to repeat it to my father. The thing . . . the news . . . is that I have a lover . . . Just that, like many matrons I have a young handsome lover. The money is for gifts . . ."

Perhaps for the first time in his life Telifrone burst out laughing. A strong, bitter laugh that shook him like a heap of echoing bones. It seemed that he would never stop. Then, becoming suddenly serious again, he said, "Foolish Cecilia. You buy the silence of the litter-bearers, but the master sent me double the amount to make them talk. In that house on the Via Appia where you go every day, where you stay into the night with your nurse, they see only poor people go in and out, ragged, toothless women, hungry children—"

"You're wrong," I interrupted weakly.

"The truth is that you have begun to frequent the Christians. That you spend your days in the company of slaves and outcasts. That you have been converted to a barbaric rite, which is alien to our traditions. And thus you insult not only me—which would be a small thing—but the name of that man who considered you worthy of receiving an education."

"Telifrone, swear to me that you won't tell him."

"You dishonor not only your father but also your husband."

"Please, Telifrone, we do no harm. We study, we pray, we do penance . . . Like you . . ."

"No, not like me. I seek God by following ancient teachings, all the wisdom contained in the books of Hermes Tris-megistos, whereas you have gone astray in a new superstition, fated to disappear in a brief time, and meanwhile you expose yourself to grave dangers. For the love I feel for you, I cannot permit it. Since I do not have the means to dissuade you, I want you to know that tomorrow I will report it to the master."

When he was on the threshold I said, "Go on, speak to my father. But one thing you should know: though I had intended to give you your freedom, I have now changed my mind."

He looked at me with sorrow and dismay, then, light as a spirit, he slipped out of the room.

I have wounded and offended someone dear to me. I used blackmail, promised revenge, with the arrogance of one who knows he is stronger. And yet if I sinned it was to protect not only myself but my brothers, your Church.

Didn't Jesus say, "Be tender as doves, sharp as serpents"?

After Hermas's rebuke, I'm confused, bewildered. My God, take me in your arms again . . . Return to me, inspire in me purity, prudence, and rectitude. Give me the grace of a vision!

I implore you, do not abandon me in my longing for you.

After the conversation with my tutor yesterday I couldn't sleep, so I woke up Carite to tell her about his threat. Maybe because she knows him better than I do, or maybe because she believes in the effectiveness of blackmail, she didn't give it too much weight, merely advising me to stop going to the community for a few days.

And now I am again confined within the walls of my house.

Even as I write, I'm continuously distracted by the anxious thoughts crowding in on me. I get up and wander through the rooms. Often, in this restless wandering, my steps lead me to Telifrone's closed door, uncertain what to do. Sometimes I have the impulse to knock, to confront him, persuade him, or maybe only be sure that he hasn't revealed the truth to my father. But something—the fear of knowing—holds me back every time.

I return to my room and, hands raised, seek repose in prayer. Yet not a word comes to my lips, which convinces me that I've lost God's love. If I read a psalm, hoping that my voice will impose a slower rhythm on the movements of my mind, I'm soon compelled to stop, because I stumble on every line. Even when I go into the garden, all I do is listen for the slightest sound that, from the atrium, could announce the arrival of my father.

Two days ago, as a penance, I began a fast that has exhausted me even more.

Today, Carite, who couldn't stand to see me in this state, decided to talk to Telifrone. She was insistent, until he agreed to open the door to her. Brusquely, without concealing the self-loathing that the resolution he had made inspired in him, he admitted he had written to the master that, after all his investigation, my behavior appeared to be blameless. Carite tried to reassure him that I'm not doing anything bad, but he said that from now on he intends to take no interest in me, and enjoined her to leave him alone.

Though the news brought relief, I nevertheless continue to torment myself for the vile way in which I obliged him to betray the trust of his beloved master. Still restless, I nag Carite to learn what the reactions of the community have been to my absence. She claims that she explained with the special prudence that my situation requires. When I remark that she hasn't been completely sincere she defends herself by maintaining that though she didn't give detailed information, she didn't lie, either. But now this shadow of duplicity increases my sense of guilt, and I will prolong the fast.

This morning, on the third day of fasting, I fainted when I got up. My nurse forced me to eat a piece of bread and some cheese, then she revealed her plan. On some pretext or other I will send Daphne to my parents: since she no longer enjoys the favor of Valerian, he will hardly notice. From now on I will do without a maid who is always around: Carite will take care of my needs. We won't go together to Petronia's house. When it's my turn I'll go out long before dawn, while she stays in my room, ready with some excuse for anyone who comes looking for me.

Then she called different litter-bearers and allowed me to return to the community.

Chia died in Petronia's arms, smiling.

Yesterday Alexander left for the Church in Antioch. Saying goodbye to me, he said, "Cecilia, take care of yourself. Remember the words of the apostle Paul, because the times are changing. 'Whether there be prophecies, they shall fail; whether there be tongues, they shall cease; whether there be knowledge, it shall vanish away. For we know in part, and we prophesy in part. But when that which is perfect is come, then that which is in part shall be done away. These then are the three things that remain: faith, hope and charity; but the greatest of all is charity.' Don't forget it, Cecilia, speak with God through charity, and in the charity of God you will find shelter."

For the first time, although I caught a note of sadness in his words, I felt that he was putting me on my guard against a danger.

When I asked him to explain he said, "Hermas defended me, it's true, but you must be cautious and modest. Don't speak to anyone about your gifts."

Then he kissed me on the cheek and went off with his wretched bundle on his shoulders. I seem to see him still, while the grief at his departure, the fear his words inspired, are still not appeased. We are alone, Lord, you and I.

I miss Alexander terribly, especially because I'm sure that today he would have come to my rescue.

We were gathered for the reading when Hermas, summoned by our bishop Eleutheros, hurried off to see him. We looked at one another, not knowing what to do, very much like lost sheep. Then, without thinking, I took the volume in my hand and began reading the account of Luke from where the presbyter had left off.

Suddenly Saturninus leaped to his feet: "Isn't it written: 'Let women be silent in the assemblies'? And Cecilia is reading the holy Gospel!"

"She doesn't even have her head covered," the wife of the presbyter added.

Each had his say. Turning in one direction, then the other, I looked at the brothers, confused and disturbed. Prisca, who is usually timid, managed to silence them and make her voice heard: "Have you forgotten the Acts of Paul and Tecla? Have you forgotten that virgin so in love with God that she refused marriage, and so dear to him that she tamed a lioness in the arena? Instead of tearing her to pieces, the beast licked her toes and killed a bear that was threatening her. When other wild beasts were sent in, Tecla jumped into a pool where fierce seals were swimming. She jumped into the pool crying, 'In the name of Jesus Christ, on this final day I am baptized!' To save her from the water monsters, God sent a lightning bolt to kill them, while the virgin emerged safe and sound from the water.

Then the magistrate let her go, and Tecla was able to join the apostle Paul, who ordered her to preach the word of God in Asia Minor . . . And she did so, enlightening many men. If a virgin can preach and even baptize herself, then, brothers, what harm can there be if Cecilia reads?"

Saturninus jumped up again: "What harm is there if she reads . . . But it's the apostle Paul himself who says that women must be submissive! That it is unlawful for them to speak! And that if they want to learn they must question their husbands at home. Because, brothers, Adam was created first and then Eve. And Adam was not deceived, but the woman, yes, she fell into sin and into sin she dragged the man, too . . ."

He was exhausted by that outburst of anger, and his last words died in his throat. I took advantage of it to say, "Saturninus, by her obedience the Virgin Mary, canceled out Eve's disobedience . . . Besides, it is written that in Christ there is no longer man or woman."

"This, yes, Paul indeed wrote!" Avilius exclaimed. "At the time when Eve was in Adam, there was no death," he said. "Death arrived when Eve was separated from him. If she again enters into him, and if he takes her with him, death will be no more. Christ came to remedy the separation that took place in the beginning, to rejoin the two, to give life to those who died because of the separation . . ."

Ishmael, a Jew who long ago converted and is now part of our community, interrupted him: "Years ago, when I was traveling in Phrygia, I heard two women preach, they were called Priscilla and Massimilla. The first claimed that Christ had appeared to her in the semblance of a woman and infused her with wisdom, revealing to her that that place was holy and that there Jerusalem would descend from Heaven. The second kept saying only, 'No more prophets will come after me, only the end . . .'"

Saturninus, who meanwhile had recovered himself and

appeared calmer, wouldn't let him continue. "Your words are blasphemous, Ishmael. Like Montano, those women were possessed by the devil, and their prophecies did not come true. As the account of Luke testifies, Jesus warns us against false prophets."

Then, taking the volume from my hand, he resumed the reading from the beginning:

"And as some spoke of the temple, how it was adorned with noble stones and offerings, he said, 'As for these things which you see, the days will come when there shall not be left here one stone upon another that will not be thrown down.'

"And they asked him, 'Teacher, when will this be, and what will be the sign when this is about to take place?'

"And he said, 'Take heed that you are not led astray; for many will come in my name, saying, "I am he!" and, "The time is at hand!" Do not go after them.

"'And when you hear of wars and tumults, do not be terrified; for this must first take place, but the end will not be at once.'

"Then he said to them, 'Nation will rise against nation, and kingdom against kingdom; there will be great earthquakes, and in various places famines and pestilences; and there will be terrors and great signs from heaven. But before all this they will lay their hands on you and persecute you, delivering you up to the synagogues and prisons, and you will be brought before kings and governors for my name's sake.'"

He bowed his head in prayer and was quickly imitated by the others. Their agitation seemed to amplify the pounding of my heart to such a point that I barely heard Apollonius utter these words: "Brothers, if God puts off the great disturbance in which the universe dissolves and, with it, every man, demon, and perverse angel, he does it for love of us and our seed. We are the only cause that moves him to spare nature. Therefore, men and women, let us all show ourselves equally worthy of his mercy."

*

"You must ask God's pardon, my daughter, because with your immodesty you have sown discord among the brothers," Hermas said to me later. "Only divine charity, certainly not knowledge, can transform your woman's weakness into strength. If you want to teach, do so by your behavior: be pure, disposed at all times to be meek and prove the moderation of your tongue by silence."

I reminded him of Esther, Judith, and all the other great women of the Books, and then the prophetess Anna, and Prisca, Paul's helper, who was able to communicate his teaching to Apollo, a Greek of vast culture.

Then, for my stubbornness, for my failure to be docile and submissive, the presbyter imposed on me two days of fasting. Silenced, I thought only of Alexander's advice, of how God allows him to justly foresee everything.

That night I had to go to a celebratory dinner at the house of the Prefect of the Games, who had just adopted Valerian.

I tried to get out of it on the pretext of a sudden illness, but my husband answered that I looked very well. Besides, since it was the third time that I had shirked my duty by refusing to go with him, he entreated me not to subject his patience to further trials, especially on such an important occasion.

So I went, but touched no food in the course of the interminable banquet, indifferent to the chatter, to the exchange of quotations, to the contests of elocution that took place around me, irritated by the eulogies that, as usual, were made to the nobility and honesty of my husband, and the filial respect he had always shown toward Portius Acilius. Every so often I felt his gaze on me, I felt the pressure of it, as if sharpened by the solidifying of a suspicion.

I observed my brother-in-law Tiburtius, who was aloof and silent, draining cup after cup. Then, suddenly, he stood up drunkenly, disrupting the scene that, for hours, had been endlessly unfolding before my eyes. He went up to his brother and raised the calyx to him. In a loud, faltering voice, he began to declaim:

Honesty is praised, but it's dying of cold.
The gardens, the palaces, the banquets,
the antique silver, the cups with goat reliefs
are the fruit of crime . . .

The guests looked at him in astonishment, whether because they had not grasped the meaning of his words or because they had caught it perfectly. Valerian, raising his cup in turn, replied with icy promptness:

Why in the world should Fabius,
even if born of the race of Hercules,
boast of the great Altar
and of ancestors who conquered the Allobrogi,
if he is greedy, lying, and more spineless
than a Euganean sheep,
if his flabby loins,
smoothed like pumice from Catania,
shame his strong ancestors,
if, buying poisons,
he dishonors his unhappy race
with an image to be smashed?

Tiburtius made a move as if to hit him, but his strength failed and he fell down. Someone laughed, while a servant helped him get up. Staggering, he left the room.

On the way home, Valerian told me he now had proof that it was his brother who had poisoned the horses before the race. Although unpleasant, the humiliation he had just inflicted had been necessary not only to counter those offensive insinuations but also to authorize the condemnation of depraved behavior that stained the family name.

Then, changing the subject, he observed that I had eaten nothing and that he found me changed, more luminous but also more distracted.

"Is there some important news that you haven't decided yet to tell me?" he added, looking into my eyes.

With a start, shaking my head violently, I exclaimed, "It's impossible!" just as I realized that that possibility was anything but remote. He insisted: "What do you mean, impossible?"

I couldn't answer because the only phrase that came to mind was "It wouldn't be my child."

I continue to think about the presbyter's rebuke, and the penance he inflicted on me, and my mind is teeming with doubts. Is he right, as Pallante, Drusus, and Telifrone were, when they accused me of weakness and lack of restraint, and of talking too much? Am I right, when I feel all the love of God? But do I feel it still, or has he abandoned me?

Today I received a letter from my father. I don't know whether I was more struck by the worsening of my mother's health or the hidden desperation with which he tells me about it.

After a period when the choking fits alternated with phases of remission, during which she resumed fasting and performing penances, she suddenly slipped into a state of stupor. She no longer speaks, and is fed by Mirrina like a baby. Like a baby taking her first steps, she walks only if supported by my father, who spends most of his time taking care of her.

"On sunny mornings," he writes, "we sit together in the garden. I read a book to her, or tell her tiny details about the day, or about the signs of advancing spring in the fields. I don't know if she can hear me. I don't know if she suffers, if behind the silence, the lethargy of her movements, the emptiness of her gaze, the suffering has retreated, concentrated into a core invisible to my eyes. Or if, on the contrary, by a sort of pitiful paradox, the soul, having surrendered its reason, has been able to yield peacefully to fate, to the arms of providence. Although my opinion changes according to moods and days, in every circumstance I thank God for having at least granted me the faculties necessary to endure events without being broken by them."

Even if he doesn't know you, my God, hear the secret prayer of my father. Receive mine, loving Father. Your daughter entreats you to save the parents you wished to give her.

They are in darkness. They tremble in fear and solitude. May the words that you inspired in the prophet Ezekiel be fulfilled: "I will give them another heart and a new spirit will I place within them; I will take away from their body the heart of stone and will give them a heart of flesh."

I can't stop thinking of my mother. How sorry I am that I so often refused to say her name, the simplest name of all: mother. Lucilla, I called her, instead, to keep her at a distance.

Ah, if Alexander were here I would take him to my mother, so that through him you might free her from despair as you did me!

Annia appeared to me in a dream. We were walking side by side, I a woman and she a child, in the Garden of Eden, just at the point where the river divides into four streams, the first of which leads to the land of gold and fragrant resin. We smelled it in the air, mixed with the odor of the beasts who came to drink or bathe in the tranquil waters. She pointed out to me the lion and the tiger, the sheep with its lamb, exclaiming each time, "Look, Mother!," a name that surprised me because I knew I was Cecilia. So I set off in search of our mother until, as I approached the bank, the reflection of my face in the water took on the features of hers.

Today Hermas forced me to publicly confess my sins. As I confessed that I had committed a sin of vanity by presuming to read before the assembly, I was burning with mortification and shame, with a sense of injustice that I couldn't stifle. When I burst into tears Apollonius embraced me.

Later, as I passed by the study, I heard him arguing with the presbyter. He said that public confessions are barbaric.

This morning I felt really ill. Still distressed by the confession, worried about my mother, unable to decipher the vision of the Garden of Eden, I sought out Apollonius in the room where he goes to study.

Not wanting to disturb him, I stood watching silently while, lying on the couch amid a pile of volumes and scrolls, he filled the sheet with rapid marks. As soon as he became aware of my presence, he sat up, then shifted some books to make room for me next to him.

I embraced him, thanking him for not leaving me alone at that difficult moment. His lips parted—perhaps he was on the point of telling me something—but he merely smiled with that gentle air that so much reminds me of my father. I told him about my father's letter, my mother's state of absence, and then I recounted the dream.

"It's not as obscure as it seems, Cecilia," he commented without hesitation. "With the metamorphosis of your face into your mother's, God has shown you the way. The water that reflected your image alludes to the rebirth in Christ through baptism, which signifies that only with the confession of faith, in every word and deed, will you be able to hope for her salvation."

Confident that he had reassured me, Apollonius smiled again and returned to his books.

Instead, by indicating an impossible task, his counsel is even more discouraging.

Ever since Hermas started reprimanding me for my vanity and my presumptuousness, and especially since Alexander's departure, I've been afraid that grace is lost forever. If God responds to my prayers with dreams or visions, their mystery, instead of calling me to him and filling me with joy as it used to, leaves me bewildered and confused, and seems to exclude me. I no longer have the certainty, even if it was arrogant, that the Spirit visits me and that I speak or sing hymns through his inspiration. I would suffer less if he hadn't so often come down to hold me in his arms. Now that he has left me, every moment is only a longing for his peace, a yearning for his presence.

Sometimes I have the impulse to go to my mother, to talk to her about Jesus, trusting in the power of his name to overcome evil. But like a wind that suddenly dies, making the sails droop, that impulse soon gives way to a melancholy inertia.

The same dark mood when I woke and arrived at the community. In the atrium Hermas's children were playing with knucklebones. The simplicity of their gestures, their childish shouts and laughter made me feel more serene, while I was reminded of Jesus's words of thanks to the Father for being revealed not to the wise, not to the learned, but to the little children, and to the young.

They were so involved in their game that they weren't aware of me, or of a stranger who, looking around shyly, entered the atrium preceded by Felix.

"He's an old friend of mine," the painter explained, approaching. "His name is Almone, and he has come to hear the word. He's a stableman at the Circus, a job that might be seen in a bad light. But I know that what leads him to the faith is pure, and now I intend to take him to Hermas and bear witness for him."

"Yes, Cecilia, it's true that I work at the Circus, but I swear to you that I have never had to perform sacrifices," the stable-man insisted on explaining.

It astonished me that he knew my name and that he addressed me as if I were an authority. Perhaps they offered these unasked-for explanations knowing that the presbyter has become more rigorous in welcoming new adherents, because of two unpleasant discoveries: Origene, who received alms reserved for the indigent, in reality earned a living making and selling amulets. And the deacon Marrius, recently summoned to help Callistus, took money from the community's funds. Since they gave no sign of repentance, Hermas expelled them both.

Lucretia is dead. I saw her die with my own eyes. I saw the anguish in hers as she fell into the darkness. I held her hands, I clasped her in my arms to hold on to her. God, don't take her away from me.

Several times in the past few days Carvilius had sent a maid to tell me how serious her condition was, but she never found me at home. This morning, I ran into her as I was going out, and immediately went with her.

I found Domitilla leaning against the wall, eyes closed, pale, arms around her already large belly. In her usual matter-of-fact way, without a sigh, she told me what had happened.

Discovering that she was pregnant, Lucretia swallowed an abortive potion that turned out to be a lethal poison. Carvilius, having consulted the best doctors, having resorted to wizards and witches, all to no purpose, had shut himself in his room, refusing to touch food.

I asked a slave if I could see him. When he returned, he reported this sentence from his master: "Dear Cecilia, I cannot." Poor man, poor Carvilius.

Yesterday in the kitchen I mended a garment, imitating Petronia's simple, precise gestures. At every pass of the needle, the torn fabric brought to life strange iridescent forms, on which I forced myself to fix my attention in order to cancel out the image of Lucretia falling into the darkness, and her frightened gaze. To erase the memory of the warm, golden light that had appeared in her eyes just a few months before, a light that, along with hope, expressed the new happiness of love, its grace, its resurrection.

My tears began to flow, dissolving the knot of pain and bewilderment that gripped my heart.

In that state of abandon I didn't notice that Avilius had entered the room.

"Why are you crying, Cecilia?" he said, appearing suddenly before me.

I don't know him very well, and I quickly dried my face with a hem of my robe.

"Why are you crying?" he repeated, and when I didn't respond he added, "I've been observing you for a while, and I recognized you. You suffer, not knowing that solitude is the fate of the chosen."

"No, Avilius. I'm crying because my best friend died in horrendous pain, she died trying to abort . . ."

"A pagan doesn't die, those who have not lived cannot die," he said. I looked at him, uncomprehending, and then Avilius tried to clarify his thought: "The brothers, and Hermas above

all, believe that the world is good because it was created by
God. But we know that they are wrong and that this world is
not the work of God but, rather, the result of a cosmic catas-
trophe. In fact it is evil, full of suffering and error, subject to
demons and archons who enslave men, keeping them in fear
and confusion, in discord and weakness. Grief at the death of
your friend includes a part of the truth, recognition of the evil
that rules over matter, but that knowledge is only the first step
toward true wisdom, which you can attain because in you the
divine spark glows. Don't let yourself be blinded, Cecilia. If
your masters say to you, 'Look, the Kingdom is in heaven,'
then the birds of the sky will precede you. If they say 'It's in the
sea,' then the fish precede you. Instead the Kingdom is within
you. When you reach the point where you know yourself, you
will understand that you are the daughter of the living Father."

"The Kingdom is within me." I continue to repeat Avilius's
words, they console me, they make me feel stronger and more
trusting. Even if I'm not sure I understand them. Just now,
though, I seem to understand a passage from the Books: "God
created the world in his image and likeness." God created me
in his image and likeness. My God, I thank you for having created me as I am. My God, forgive my friend.

Events have happened so quickly that I haven't had a moment to write.

A week ago, after spending the whole day with Petronia caring for the sick, I came home late at night. I was so tired I didn't even feel the usual fear that someone had noticed my absence. But waiting for me in my room was Valerian.

His voice trembling with anger, he asked where I had been until that hour and where I went every day, stealing his money. Then, without giving me time to answer, and in a suddenly calm tone that was even more frightening, he admitted that he had been mistaken about me. He had never considered me very obedient or respectful, I was impulsive, but he would not have suspected that I could harbor the duplicity of an adulterer.

"It's not true!" I cried. My denial was so sincere that it cloaked with truth the lie that came to my lips without my thinking about it.

"Every day I go to the temple of Isis. And sometimes I stay at night. The money I use for offerings."

He laughed—that laugh quiet and rhythmic as a sigh, which, however, could not hide the relief, the danger of a greater evil avoided. How weak he is, ready to believe any lie to protect his image.

With an air of contempt he resumed. "You're a fool, Cecilia. And maybe I'm a fool, too, not to realize that, though you've been absent recently, no man would notice you. Be careful you don't get sick, with all the fasting you do."

When he left I stood leaning on the door for I don't know how long, incapable of the slightest movement. I asked God's forgiveness for lying, then I remembered the vision in which my face became my mother's, and I thought that he had wanted to suggest to me how to answer Valerian. In confusion I gave thanks to him for having inspired that lie. Immediately afterward, in a flash of lucidity, I again asked his forgiveness for daring to think such a blasphemous thought.

"You believe that I have come to bring peace on earth? No, I say to you: rather, division": I heard again the words of Jesus, now sure that the presbyter was wrong, and that to follow Jesus's teaching I would soon have to break with anyone—father or husband—who was an obstacle on that path.

The next day I asked Carite to get me a black shawl like the one that the worshippers of Isis wear, and, overcoming my repulsion, I tied it under my breast. In order not to rekindle Valerian's suspicions, I stayed home and managed to see him in the atrium.

"Be careful not to get caught in the great whore's sistrum," he said, with a mocking glance at the fringe that touched my feet.

I waited for him to go ahead of me into the street, then I went out, making sure that his litter had left before going to the alley where mine was waiting.

A fire forced us to make a detour, so that the journey took longer, and by the time I reached Petronia's house the brothers had already gathered. Approaching the room, I heard the sometimes harsh, sometimes sorrowful sounds of a violent argument. No one seemed to notice when I entered, apart from Almone, the new adherent, who gave me a furtive, almost frightened glance. I sat down beside Apollonius, while the deacon Callistus accused Avilius:

"You shamelessly call yourselves perfect, boasting that you have more than what is contained in the Gospel. You even dare to call the gospel of truth some recent writing of yours: it is so different from the Gospels of the apostles that even the term 'gospel' is profaned. In fact, if yours is the gospel of truth and is different from that of the apostles, it is evident that it cannot be the gospel of truth . . . Further, you dare to assert that the son of God was not incarnated and, contradicting yourselves, maintain that Jesus Christ seems, but is not, a man, and even that Christ entered Jesus during baptism and left him on the Cross."

"Don't you hear the living Jesus laughing on the Cross?" Avilius replied. "Because he in whose hands and feet they stick nails is only his physical wrapping, his substitute. They dishonor only what resembles him, and he laughs at their stupidity! The flesh is nothing, nothing but a trap for spirits who, like you, still wander in error and oblivion."

Red in the face with anger, Callistus turned to the gathering: "Brothers, they bear the name of Christians, while they think and do things prohibited by God. According to them, we of the Church are supposed to be psychic men. And as such we are brought up with psychic things, confirmed through works and an ingenuous faith, without perfect knowledge. So for us good conduct is necessary, otherwise there is no salvation. They, on the other hand, are saved not through works but because they are spiritual by nature. Like gold tossed in the mud they do not lose their shine, so—they say—no matter what material work they devote themselves to, they cannot be damaged or lose their spiritual nature. Those whom they consider perfect therefore commit without scruples all forbidden acts: they eat meat sacrificed to idols, they secretly corrupt women, they engage in the most unrestrained fornication in what they call the marriage chamber. You must avoid them like people infected with an incurable disease."

"You, who call yourselves bishops, presbyters, and deacons, as if you had received authority from God, are nothing but dried-up rivers."

"They are mad dogs who bite secretly. Brothers, let us hunt them like fierce beasts," Callistus lashed out, beside himself. And he ordered Avilius to leave and not be seen again. Avilius rose and exploded in a powerful laugh. I could still hear it echoing in the atrium after he disappeared.

As the deacon walked up and down struggling to master himself, we looked at each other in dismay and bewilderment, without saying a word. Finally he stopped and asked us to come together in prayer.

I recited mechanically, upset by that exchange of insults, when the presbyter entered the room and Callistus interrupted us to recount to him what had happened. After praising his rigor, Hermas warned, "He who does not recognize that Jesus Christ came in flesh is an anti-Christ; and he who does not recognize the sacrifice of the Cross is on the side of the devil; and he who adapts the teachings of the Lord to his own desires, denying the Resurrection and the Judgment, is the firstborn of Satan."

Avilius an anti-Christ, a dissolute who corrupts women. To me he was an affectionate brother, who only wanted to comfort me! Those with knowledge, the firstborn of Satan, while they pray like us and practice fasting even more severe than ours. Suddenly, in the accusations of the deacon and the presbyter I felt the poison of lies. I was on the point of speaking in defense of Avilius when Gaius, the presbyter's oldest son, burst in crying that the emperor Marcus Aurelius was dead.

That same day I wrote to Telifrone to tell him that I intended to free him.

My God, help me, give me courage. Soon they will come . . .

Already I seem to hear their heavy steps approaching. But even in a cell there is always a crack, a patch of sky to look at, and enough space in my heart to raise my hands in prayer. Only let me not find myself in the same prison as Hermas and Callistus!

My Father, do not abandon me.

They have allowed me to bring one change of clothes, a towel, pen, ink, and a pile of papyruses. How many are there? To them I confide my thanks to the Lord for testing me and a prayer to keep me strong so that, as the dream about the Garden of Eden foretold, the resolution to confess the name of Jesus may save my mother.

Only now do I understand the simplest thing, the truest: one must have the courage to say that one believes, one must dare to utter the name of God.

The cell is dark. Telifrone paid the guards to put a small lamp at my disposal, but the light is barely sufficient to illuminate the papyrus. In exchange, I hear every sound, as if amplified by the subterranean vaults. I hear the voices and laments of the other prisoners, packed by the dozens into the same cramped space, the women—healthy or sick—crowded into a damp, mice-infested cave. I glimpsed them as they led me to this cell reserved for nobles, the only one provided with a pallet, a basin, and a pitcher of water.

Perhaps because of the intense cold I've lost my voice. I pray in my soul. I pray for Almone, the Circus stableman who informed on me. For Tiburtius, who instigated him to join the community in order to gather the necessary evidence against me. For Carite, who, not wanting to leave me alone, wished to surrender to the authorities, and is now desperate for having let herself be dissuaded by our bishop Eleutherius. When she comes to see me all she does is weep and tremble. My God, I pray you, do not abandon her.

I pray for my father, whom Telifrone informed and who will soon arrive. For my mother, I entreat you to keep her in her absent state, far from this new suffering.

For the soul of Lucretia, I call on your mercy. Out of love you wished your son to become a man. She, too, bore her small cross.

I don't know which magistrate will be responsible for my interrogation and when it will take place. In this uncertainty, I find comfort only in the visits of some of the brothers. Petronia's generosity persuaded my jailers to give them free access day and night. After Carite, today Hermas and his wife came to see me. He seemed uneasy: that the confession of faith is entrusted to someone like me is troublesome for him. He asked if I felt strong enough to sustain it. I had the impulse to throw him out, but you, my God, tied my tongue and then you loosened it, and I invited him to pray with me. Later Felix came to see me, weeping as he begged me to forgive him. He had known Almone from childhood, he trusted him, he had even testified that he should be welcomed into the community. He, however . . . "He believed he could destroy the most beautiful flower of God . . . my little flower," he added, turning violently red. Then he prostrated himself to kiss my feet. Before he left he painted a dove on the wall to imbue me with the strength of the Spirit.

Maybe because of the darkness, or more likely the distance that separates us, when Valerian entered the cell I didn't recognize him. I rose from the pallet, narrowing my eyes in order to focus.

"You know, Cecilia," he began in a faint, almost absent-minded voice, "after my father's death I had second thoughts about marrying you. From our meetings I had acquired doubts about your character. In the sweetness of your gaze I glimpsed an abandon, behind your liveliness the shadow of fanaticism.

Then, in your intelligence, the seed of obstinacy. But it was easier to follow the mirage that your grace offered me . . . And
now, confirming my suspicions, you have joined this third race
of wretched, fanatic, and superstitious people. You call brother any crude, vulgar shoemaker, brother in a stupid faith that
appeals to slaves, women, children, and fools, promising them
the kingdom of God. You who are beautiful, who grew up
amid beauty, now boast that you despise it. It is said that you
worship a god who died on the cross. That he knew what his
destiny would be. But what god, what demon, what man of
sense, if he had known from the beginning that such things
would happen to him, would not have tried to avoid them,
rather than throw himself into what he already knew? What
madness! What a repulsive and outrageous idea. I wonder how
you can believe in such nonsense, but in the end it has nothing
to do with me. Worship whatever god you prefer. Only be sure
not to complete the revenge that my brother has plotted to dishonor me, by refusing to deny Almone's accusation. Since I
can hardly believe that you are guilty of the crimes that the
people charge you with, and since the justice of Rome is magnanimous, it will suffice for you to sacrifice to Caesar to regain
your dignity and mine, which you have seriously compromised.
For now this is all I ask."

My God, I loved him so much, let him also find you! Like
all my future enemies, I seem to see them already, blinded by
anger and contempt. I beg you to inspire me with the right
words so that I may respond with humility to their proud
speeches, with prayers to their curses, with faith to their error,
with meekness to their cruelty.

Suddenly the laments stopped, the guards' footsteps faded.
In the silence I hear the chirping of a sparrow. Annia's sparrow? The sound of God startles me.

*

The Lord has given me the grace of a vision, in which I appeared strong and calm while a magistrate interrogated me. Beside me was Quintus, who clasped my hand, as he did that day at the river to seal our pact of friendship. On waking I understood that my repentance had been accepted, and with a heart full of gratitude I prayed God to give me the courage to face my father.

"Think not that I am come to bring peace on earth: I came not to bring peace, but a sword. For I am come to set a man at variance against his father, and the daughter against her mother, and the daughter-in-law against her mother-in-law. And a man's foes shall be they of his own household. He that loveth father or mother more than me is not worthy of me; and he that loveth son or daughter more than me is not worthy of me. And he that taketh not his cross, and followeth after me, is not worthy of me."

He came today. His hair is white now, he is bent under the weight of suffering.

But his gaze was the same, clear and firm. Rising to meet him, I hesitated.

"Don't be afraid, I'm not going to test your new faith with entreaties and laments. I won't ask you to have pity on my old age, or on your father, though it's true that I am worthy of being called father by you and though it's true that I brought you to maturity with my own hands. Nor will I ask you to think of my name. Of the shame, the mockery, the dishonor to which you expose it. No, I wish to appeal not to an affection that you evidently don't feel but to a faculty to whose development I devoted all possible care, in spite of your sex, and which now you give proof of insulting, accepting a doctrine without being guided by reason. 'Don't question, have faith,' the Christians say, or, 'Your faith will save you.' A certain Paul of Tarsus in fact states, 'Where is the wise man? Where is the learned man? Where is the subtle reasoner of this world? Has not God demonstrated the wisdom of this world to be foolish?' As in other superstitions, the Christians refuse to give or receive an account of the object of their belief, and exalt as a good in itself the blindness of faith. I only want you to answer me, to tell me how it could happen that such attitudes have won you over to the point that you are willing to put your life in danger to defend them."

"God saved me. I was dead, in spirit and body, and he appeared to me in all his light, in all his love . . . That God whose name you do not know was manifested through his Son, who died on the Cross to wash away our sins and give us eternal life."

"You continue to reject judgment, or any appeal to reason."

"You know Apollonius—he would be able to show you. And I, too, might be able to. I could tell you that many truths claimed by the philosophers come from our Books, that Plato took from the words of the prophets the idea that the Lord made the world, shaping formless matter, and the Stoics, too, because of their moral teaching, inspired by the Word, were persecuted and put to death. Still, I became a Christian not by learning these truths but because God called me to him, gave me grace and eternal life. Turning to him as his daughter, I became like him."

"No, you do not resemble him, because you have a body. However, like a true father, God made you a gift of something of himself, and that is of all the faculties enabling you to live according to reason. And he gave them freely, without restrictions or impediments, making them depend on you, without keeping for himself any power that might obstruct or limit them. You, however, believe that in his perfection God needs you. That, because you are born of him, equal to him, all things are subject to you, the earth and the water and the air and the stars, and everything is made for you and ordered to serve you. Do you really believe you are so important, Cecilia?"

I used to lose myself in music, now I lose myself in God.

My sight is weakening and writing has become painful. Worried about fire, the jailers won't allow me to use another lamp. I asked my tutor to ask one of them, named Ierax: he's a kind man. Yesterday he said to me, "I know that you do no harm. Over there is someone else who says he's a Christian. His name is Saturus, he is pious and generous and cares for his cellmates, with whom he shares everything that's brought from home."

Telifrone has gone to live with my father in the house in Trastevere. He sees him struggling from morning to night in his search for help. So little time has passed since he gave up the post of Prefect of the Annona, and yet already everyone seems to have forgotten him: the master's affairs are no longer of interest to anyone, he commented bitterly.

Gaius Publius Primus, his onetime protector, is dead. Some, learning of my imprisonment, refuse to receive him. Others limit themselves to counseling the only road that seems possible, which is that I deny the name of Jesus and sacrifice to the emperor and the gods.

What further complicates the situation, according to my pedagogue, and makes the authority and the jurisdictions more uncertain and confusing, is the fact that Marcus Aurelius didn't have time to appoint a successor to the Prefect of the City, who died in a fall from a horse, and that neither Commodus nor the Prefect of the Praetorian has yet returned from Germany. The magistrate who will conduct the interrogation has not been named, so my father doesn't know where to go to get permission for me, as a noble, to be kept under guard at home.

Telifrone also mentioned a certain rescript in which the Emperor Hadrian established that if someone made an accusation against the Christians, showing that they acted against the law, the judge would have to decide, based on the seriousness of the crime, to punish an accuser who lodged a complaint for the purpose of calumny. Since the definition of the crime is vague, that leaves a broad margin of action and interpretation to the magistrate: in the end cases are entrusted to his discretionary power. Not to mention that, far from helping to lighten the punishment, my rank could make it worse.

He concluded, "If you don't sacrifice to the emperor, you'll be guilty of impiety and a crime against the ruler. But Rome is tolerant: saving yourself depends on you alone, Cecilia."

To Apollonius, who came to see me today, I said that my greatest terror is that I won't pass the test. "The test will come for all of us," he answered.

As I followed Ierax, who was leading me to the magistrate Almachius for the interrogation, I repeated the words of Jesus: "But when they deliver you up, take no thought how or what ye shall speak: for it shall be given you in that same hour what ye shall speak. For it is not ye that speak, but the Spirit of your Father which speaketh in you."

"What is your name?"

"My first name is that of Christian, but if you want to know my name in this world, I am Cecilia Clara."

"What is your condition?"

"I am a Roman citizen, of noble family."

"But I want to know what religion you are."

"This interrogation is starting badly; you're not listening to my answers."

"Where do you get such arrogance?"

"From a true faith."

"Don't you know what power I have?"

"It's you who don't know: if you asked me I would tell you."

"Tell me, then."

"Any power of man is like a goatskin full of air: if you take a needle and make a small hole, the goatskin deflates in an instant."

"You began with insults and in insults you persist."

"I learned to pray, not to proffer insults."

"You don't know that our princes have ordered that anyone who confesses to be a Christian be condemned and that anyone who declares he no longer wishes to be so should be set free? And they have made that decision only because they are merciful, and wish to safeguard the good of your life."

"If someone is accused of being a Christian, even if it turns out that he is innocent, you immediately condemn him, only because he is Christian. We, instead, knowing that being a Christian is a holy thing, do not for any reason wish to say that we are not Christians. Indeed, it is better to die happily than to live unhappily, but this truth tortures you judges, and you would prefer to hear us lie."

"Choose: sacrifice to the gods and to the good fortune of the Emperor Commodus, or say you are not a Christian, so you will be able to return home."

"I do not recognize the Empire of this world; rather, I serve that God whom no man has seen or can see with these eyes."

"Almone is ready to testify that you are a Christian and that you follow their wicked practices: if you will say you are not, you will put an end to the charge; in the opposite case, your own foolishness, and not I, will be the cause of your condemnation."

"That Almone should charge me is what I desire, and the punishment to which you condemn me will be my victory."

"You're mad! Don't you know that the princes have granted me the power of life and death? How do you dare to speak with such pride?"

"It's one thing to be proud, another to be consistent: I have spoken with consistency, not pride. If you are not afraid to hear the truth, I will tell you that you, a short time ago, said something very false."

"What did I say that was false?"

"You claim that you have been granted the authority to give life and condemn to death, while you know perfectly that you have only the power to give death: indeed, you can give death to the living but you cannot give life to the dead.

"I do not consider it terrible to die for the true God, because what I am, I am through his work, and I would endure anything rather than deserve eternal death: whether living or dead, I am a thing of God."

"And thinking thus, Cecilia, you are happy to die?"

"Truly I am happy to live, but not so much as to fear death for love of life. Nothing is more precious than life, yes, but eternal life."

"Stop being so arrogant and sacrifice to the gods."

"I see only rocks, brass, and lead. I worship instead the God who is in the Heavens, and to him alone I bow my head, to him who instills in every man a living spirit and who every day causes life to flow in each of us. And I will not prostrate myself to worship dead idols, the work of woodcarvers, goldsmiths, and potters, who have ears and do not hear, have eyes and do not see, have hands and do not reach out, have feet and do not walk. And are thus the image itself of the lie."

"You wretch! All you Christians are wretches! If you want to die there are plenty of ditches to throw yourselves in and ropes with which to hang yourselves! Give yourselves death and you will join your god, without any trouble. In spite of your folly, through the magnanimity of Caesar, and through regard for your rank, I grant you six days to reflect. But, because of the arrogance you have demonstrated, you will spend them here and not in your own house."

Then Almachius ordered the guards to lead me back to my cell.

C arite visited me with Avilius. I was surprised that he came to see me after being expelled from the community, but soon I understood that my nurse had sought him out. She is losing her faith and no longer knows how to persuade me to deny the name of Christ.

Avilius said, "Here you are, too, Cecilia, ready to follow in the footsteps of those fools who think that confessing 'We are Christians,' in words and not in deeds, and, giving themselves up to a human death, without knowing where they're going, without even knowing who Christ is, are convinced that they will live! If words of testimony were sufficient for salvation, the whole world would submit to this formality, and all of us would be saved. Instead they lose themselves, since only a god puffed up with pride could claim a human sacrifice. The martyrs, then, like their false masters, await the resurrection of the flesh, not knowing that, through the power of God, the true resurrection, on the contrary, consists in its end. Don't let the shadows obscure you, Cecilia, don't deliver yourself to ignorance!"

At first Carite sat uneasily, her head bent, tormented by guilt, but after a while she looked up at him with an incredulous gaze, as if in irritation. Finally, unable to contain herself, she exclaimed, "Avilius, how can you think of convincing her, if not a word of what you're saying is comprehensible!" I laughed. How long since that had happened? Then I said to Avilius that even if I wanted to save myself I couldn't ignore the fact that if I don't go, someone else will have to go in my place. Therefore one must have the courage to utter the name of Jesus.

Telifrone brought me a letter from Domitilla:

"My friend,

I learned with distress the news of your imprisonment from Sextus. I would make the journey from Mantua to see you but the doctor has ordered me not to leave my bed. I don't know these Christians you've joined, or if the atrocious accusations that are made against them are true—that they sacrifice and eat babies or engage in incestuous relations—but I am ready to testify in writing that I know you are just and pure and that such behavior on your part is in not credible.

Be strong, do not despair, and tell me if I can help you in any way."

In great anxiety and confusion, and no longer knowing what earthly remedy to resort to, Carite said to me, "My child, you are so deserving that you can ask for the grace of a vision, to know if you are truly destined for martyrdom or if you will be saved."

I felt sorry for her and would have preferred not to respond. But she was so insistent that I promised her to ask for that grace. That same night I had a vision.

I saw a very high bronze stairway that reached to the sky, but it was narrow and only one person at a time could climb it. All types of iron tools were attached to the sides of the stairway: there were swords, lances, harpoons, long knives, spits, so that if you climbed carelessly or failed to look upward, you would get mangled, with your flesh caught on the iron. At the foot of the stairway lay an extraordinarily large serpent that waited at the entrance for anyone who approached, to frighten him and prevent his ascent. In front of me went Saturus, the brother in the cell next to mine, although I've never met him. Reaching the top of the stairway, he turned and said, "Cecilia, I'm waiting for you. But take care that the serpent doesn't bite you." I answered, "He will do nothing to me, in the name of Jesus." Indeed the serpent slowly raised its head, as if it feared me. Then, treading on its head as if it were the first step, I began to climb. And I saw an immense garden, and sitting in the middle of it was a very tall white-haired man, in shepherd's garb, who was milking some sheep; and all around was a great crowd dressed in white. The old man looked up and said, "Welcome, daughter." Then he called me by name and offered me a bite of cheese. I took it with joined hands and ate it, while all those present said, "Amen."

At the sound of those voices I woke, still chewing something sweet.

I didn't want to tell Carite the vision, but again she was so insistent that I couldn't avoid it, and she immediately understood that it meant martyrdom. Angry at me, she uttered terrible words: "What is this cruel God who can wish for the sacrifice of an innocent?" She left the cell without looking at me.

Telifrone told me that Valerian, learning of the outcome of the interrogation, informed my father of his intention to divorce me. My God, I thank you for having relieved me of a marriage in which I see nothing but a useless burden. I will go to you lighter.

Then he told me that my father, in his tireless efforts to save me, met Julius, who was visiting Rome. By what to him seems a very lucky coincidence, my uncle has known Almachius since childhood and in the name of that friendship will ask him to at least allow me to be under guard at home in Trastevere. My pedagogue added that, although he does not want it noticed, the master is suffering terribly both for me and for my mother, who has not left her bed since his departure for Rome.

He bitterly reproached me for my lack of piety. As for him, he is guilt-ridden at his betrayal of my father's trust, at having concealed the truth from him when it was not yet too late. With eyes full of tears he took a step toward me, perhaps to embrace me, then fled.

I am again in the house of my childhood, with my father, Carite, and Telifrone. Outside the door of my room are two guards, but I can go in and out as I please.

In the garden, spring has arrived. In the hottest hours I sit observing the tips of the cypresses waving in the wind, and listen to the gushing of the fountain. My God, I thank you for every breath, for this soft air that caresses my face. I beg you to keep me strong, so that the announcement of salvation contained in the vision of the Garden of Eden may come true.

The first swallows dot the sky. I remember the song of the children of Rhodes that Telifrone taught me as a child.

> See the little swallow,
> who brings fine days,
> who brings on its wings
> a year of marriages,
> white-bellied swallow,
> black-and-silver mantled.

I sing softly, with a desperate yearning for my dear ones and for this garden, the air, the cypresses, all that surrounds me and that I am about to leave.

Seeing my father grieves me. Seeing his red eyes, with their dark circles, the deep wrinkles carved in his forehead. Since my arrival he hasn't spoken a single word to me. When we meet he goes straight on, looking away. I can do nothing for him, only pray.

From Telifrone I know that he wrote a petition to Commodus asking that, in the event that I am obstinate and refuse to deny my faith, the Emperor may be merciful and commute the death sentence into exile.

But time is urgent, and Almachius, whom my father has visited, is said to be extremely angry at my insolence. In his eyes, as Telifrone predicted, my nobility worsens the insult to Caesar and to Rome, and he is said to be ready to apply the law in an inflexible manner.

He forbade me to receive visits at home, but yesterday by paying the guards Apollonius, Petronia, and Callistus were able to come. Even if seeing the deacon gave me no relief, we all prayed together. Then, in the desire to strengthen my faith, he recalled the example of Blandina, who was tied to a stake and exposed to wild beasts.

The deacon then quoted a passage of the letter of Ignatius to the Romans, in which he urges the brothers to do nothing to avoid martyrdom: "Let me instead be given as food for the beasts, through whom I can reach the Lord. I am the grain of God, and under the grinding of their teeth I wish to become the immaculate bread of Christ. Therefore rather caress the beasts, that they may give me a grave in their belly, and leave nothing of my body . . ."

Petronia's eyes were closed, her face contracted in an expression of grief. For my part, I made a vain effort to control the shudder that ran through my body. Perhaps Apollonius noticed and, interrupting the deacon, invited us again to join in prayer.

Today, on the eve of the second interrogation, my father wished to see me. As he entered the room, he began to speak, without looking at me: "You know that I am not opposed to voluntary death when such a gesture derives from an individual, well-considered, and serious reflection. The house is full of smoke? I'll go out, knowing that the door is always open. Instead, your readiness to die, like that of all the Christians, is based on pure and simple opposition. Inspired by an ignoble impulse, not by a reasoned judgment, it is theatrical, completely external, and so not convincing to others. Not even to those who, like me in fact, are disposed to admit in certain cases the reasonableness of such a choice. Yet if you think you have some argument in its favor, I am willing to listen to you."

My indifference to his words pained me, as if my father and I were now strangers to one another, aliens who speak different languages without any possibility of understanding.

Yet though he is, like me, aware of this, he still hoped to persuade me, and waited silently for my response. When I said nothing, he resumed as if to himself, "Sometimes I say to myself that if I had a right to read your diary I would understand that you were incapable of going forward by yourself and that I had to save you by force . . . Last night God gave me a dream in which you appeared lying on one side, your head bound in a cloth, and your face turned away, as if to hide from my gaze. A light breath seemed to animate your breast, so I approached quietly, in order not to wake you, but as soon as I touched you I realized that you had been transformed into a statue of Parian marble, whose whiteness gave off an intense cold. I leaned over to warm you with my breath, to melt the hardness of the stone into pulsing flesh. Only then, in the grip of anguish, did I notice three deep cuts in your neck."

This morning, at the deadline of the sixth day, Almachius came to interrogate me.

"Have you reflected, Cecilia? You may merit the Emperor's clemency if you change your mind."

"I am a Christian, I have nothing else to add," I replied, as I thought again of the wish that Telifrone had addressed to me concluding the story of his life: "May Fortune always be kind to you, Cecilia! May you never find yourself in the situation of losing the possession you consider most precious! But if through ill fortune that should happen, may the gods give you the strength to preserve and defend it, unlike what I did."

Reading the sentence, which was engraved on a tablet, Almachius decreed that tomorrow I should be decapitated. As a gesture of pity and respect for my father, however, he allowed me to spend the last night in his house.

Then he commanded the guards to lead me back to my room and not let me emerge until the moment of execution.

My God, give me a new life, where the smallest things, the most beautiful things, are vast and eternal.

I'm trembling all over, devastated. Rage possesses me—against Carite, Telifrone, my father. Above all against my father, who barred the way to you, my God. As I write I repeat your name, I repeat it again and again to find some peace, my God.

In the garden that surrounds the villa I recognized the roses and, in the distance, the hills with the majestic oak and the peach trees in flower.

I heard a noise behind me, and, turning slowly, mind and body pervaded by a strange torpor, I found myself in the arms of my nurse. She was weeping, laughing, and, struggling between happiness and remorse, she asked my forgiveness, shaking me hard to make me understand that it was not a dream, that it really was the two of us in flesh and blood.

Then she told me that the night before the execution, while the guards were sleeping, my father entered the room and administered a mandrake powder, which induces apparent death in the body. At dawn he had asked if he could say a final farewell and, finding me lifeless on the bed, had written to Almachius to come with a doctor to confirm my death . . . I didn't let her finish, I escaped and shut myself in my room.

I felt an overwhelming desire to see my mother.

She was lying in bed, her gaze opaque, pale.

"Mother," I said, taking her in my arms. "Do you recognize me? Please, mother, say my name," and I moved away so that she could look at me. She stared at me without saying a word, without expression. Then I covered her face with kisses. "I love you so much, mother," I said, weeping. She closed her eyes, as if overcome by weariness. When I hugged her again I felt her hand resting gently on my cheek.

Cecilia."

I was absorbed in prayer, and I didn't immediately recognize his voice.

"Cecilia," my father called me again.

I turned toward him, slowly, not daring to look at him.

"Carite and Telifrone did not betray you. If it's a question of guilt in your eyes, I am ready to take upon myself the whole weight."

I said nothing, eyes fixed on the ground.

He resumed, "You know . . . with the vision in which you showed me the fatal wounds on your neck, God indicated to me my task. Thus, violating the laws of Rome, I resolved to do what depended on me and my freedom."

I look at the fresco beside the bed: the yellow of the pomegranates on the branches, the flutter of a turtle dove's wings among leaves stirred by the wind, and, half hidden by a tuft of grass, the white rabbit, almost identical to the one I played with as a child. The garden is fenced in. The circle is closed again. Outside doesn't exist. Perhaps it never existed. Rome does not exist, nor I for it.

We can receive nothing that was not assigned to us by Heaven.

My God, we must say that we believe, feel you living in our heart, in every instant, now . . . We must endure your mysteries, abandon ourselves to your embrace, say that we want to live . . .

"Give me a new life, where the smallest things, the most beautiful, are vast and eternal." At least for a moment. My God, you answered my prayer.

I went to find Marta in the meadow, she whom I had so feared to see in all these years. But under the oak were two young slaves I didn't know. Then I went to the slaves' quarters. I went through the rooms asking for my friend. They showed me a dark room, and for a moment I was afraid. First, crossing the threshold, I distinguished nothing in all that darkness. Then I heard a faint cry coming from a corner and I approached. On a mattress Marta was nursing twins. She looked up and smiled at me, passionately happy. She took one of the babies from her breast and held him out to me. When I bent over to take him she said his name. She said, "Quintus."

Lord, we must trust you with humility, accept your miracles: the dream you gave my father about my lifeless body, life that I wanted and that you wished to give me again.

"The Kingdom is within you," Avilius said to me.

Paradise is the lost garden. It is this garden.

There will be my mother: drawing from a deep spring, perhaps she will utter my name. I will hear the calm voice of my father, I will recognize the footsteps of Telifrone and Carite's odor of milk. We will free Marta. I will help her bring up the twins and teach them to read and write. I'll talk to them of Jesus. I'll sing them the song of the children of Rhodes.

I'll see these roses, and in the distance the hills with the majestic oak. In the silence of my heart there will also be simple things and fragments of eternity.

Author's Note

This novel originated in a love affair, one of many that Cecilia has continued to inspire through the centuries, spinning out legends, amplifying the myth.

A Roman girl of noble family who converts to Christianity.

And then, through a mistake in interpretation of a passage in the legend devoted to her, that girl becomes the patron saint of musicians.

A slender white figure sculpted in marble fourteen centuries later by a twenty-year-old artist, Stefano Maderno. In the candlelit basilica, he was left alone, day and night, with the body of Cecilia, which had just been exhumed from the crypt. A silent yet remarkable dialogue between two young people, between life and death, between art and faith.

Sade was struck by this statue during his journey to Rome: "A truth so devastating rules this divine work that it is impossible not to be moved by it. Cecilia was small but delicate . . . a beautiful flower cut down just as it was about to bloom . . ."

Even today the basilica in Trastevere dedicated to her is filled with worshipers, embroidered cloths, and red roses on November 22, her feast day.

ACKNOWLEDGMENTS

Thanks to Laura Gonsalez, who has always been my guide.

To my mother, Barbara, Eva, Maurizio, Sandra, and Sandro. To Lorena Camerini, Antonietta De Lillo, Emma Fattorini, Elisabetta Lodoli, Dario Nicoletti, Sandro Parone, Giuseppe Piccioni, Marc Sémo, Maria and Candide Soci, Domenico Starnone.

Thanks for the colors and the new notes that each of you gave Cecilia.

Thanks to Caterina Serra, for not leaving me alone, for your passionate readings and your deep, watchful gaze.

To Valerio, thanks for your "hmmm . . ."s.

Thanks to Eva Cantarella and Claudio Ceciarelli for their valuable advice.

Thanks to Enrico: without you there would have been no beginning.

And to Marco Vigevani and Cynthia Cannell, for having given me confidence. It takes many people, and a lot of love, to make a book.

Bibliographical Note

Acts of the Martyrs of Gaul, Acts of the Martyrdom of Apollonius, in *Acts of the Martyrs*.

Aelius Aristides, *To Rome*.

Aelius Aristides, *Sacred Tales*.

Apuleius, *Metamorphoses (The Golden Ass)*.

Catullus, *Odes*.

Celsus, *The True Word*.

Didache, or *Teaching of the Twelve Apostles*.

Epictetus, *Diatribes and Fragments*.

Epictetus, *Manual*.

Eusebius of Caesarea, *Ecclesiastical History*.

The Gospel of Truth, the Gospel of Philip, from the Gnostic Gospels.

The Gospel According to Matthew, the Gospel According to Luke.

Horace, *Odes and Epodes*.

Irenaeus of Lyons, *Against Heresies*.

Irenaeus of Lyons, *Epideixis*.

Justinian, *Apologies*.

Juvenal, *Satires*.

Lucian, *Fantastic Stories (The Ship or The Wishes; Icaromenippus or The Sky-man; The Dead Come to Life or The Fisher-*

man; *The Lover of Lies, or The Doubter; Timon or The Misanthrope; A True Story*).

Lucretius, *De Rerum Naturae.*

Marcus Aurelius, *Meditations.*

Martial, *Epigrams.*

Ovid, *The Art of Love.*

Ovid, *The Metamorphoses.*

The Passion of Saints Perpetua and Felicity.

Pliny the Younger, *Letters.*

Plutarch, *Dialogue on Love.*

Plutarch, *Isis and Osiris.*

Priscilla and Domitilla, *Prophecies.*

St. Clement of Rome, *Letter to the Corinthians.*

St. Ignatius, *Letters.*

St. Paul, *Letters.*

Seneca, *Consolations.*

Seneca, *Letters to Lucilius.*

The Shepherd of Hermas.

The Testimony of Truth, Nag Hammadi Codex IX 3.

Virgil, *Aeneid.*

De Rossi, G. B., *Roma sotterranea* [*Underground Rome*], Rome 1864, 1867.

Santa Cecilia martire romana: Titulus Caeciliae Centro di spiritualità liturgica.

Iscrizioni funerarie romane [*Roman Funerary Inscriptions*], edited by L. Storoni Mazzolani, BUR 2000.

Pighi, G. P., *Supplica a Giunone Regina* [*Prayer to Queen Juno*], in *Giochi secolari del popolo romano dei Quiriti.* Amsterdam, 1965.

Linda Ferri is the author of the novel *Enchantments*, a collection of short stories, and numerous books for children. She cowrote the films *The Son's Room* (Palme d'Or 2001, Cannes), directed by Nanni Moretti; *The Life I Want* and *Light of My Eyes*, directed by Giuseppe Piccioni; and *Along the Ridge*, directed by Kim Rossi Stuart. She lives in Rome.